# Mark Vardy
# and the
# School of Ninjas

# DEDICATION

To Rod, my Sensei, my inspiration and the original Mark Vardy.

To Grandmaster Brian Dossett, who launched a fleet of thousands.

To the memory of Professor Bob Lawrence, who first showed me the magic of Martial Arts.

To all the Senseis who give so much to so many.

# ACKNOWLEDGMENTS

The author would like to thank Rod Walton for sharing his imagination, his Martial Arts expertise and decades of experience in the Police Force. Thank you also for the many conversations in which you helped me plan this book and your unfailing enthusiasm and belief in me.

Thanks are also due to the friends and family of the author who so kindly read various drafts of this first Mark Vardy book and gave so much encouragement and support. Thank you to Helen Knight, Norma Goater, David Bennett, Karen Teulon, Bernard Witcher and Dawn Willock.

Thanks also to Lauren Raybould for her editing services.

A book like this – and those which will follow – could not have been written without so many generations of Martial Artists sharing and handing down their knowledge. I hope I have done them justice and will do so even more in the future. But I must at least acknowledge what they have given all of us.

Finally, thank you to the New Forest, the scene of much of this book and the place of daily inspiration to the author.

## Chapter 1

"Mark?" His mother called out of the kitchen door out into the garden with amused resignation. "Mark? Have you got Geoff in your prison? I've got Mrs Jones at the door and it's time for his tea."

"I can't let him out yet Mum," Mark replied. "He's in for criminal damage."

At seven years old, Mark was quite convinced he was a police officer and considered it his duty to police the activities of the neighbourhood children.

"Criminal damage can wait until tomorrow Mark. Let him out," she said firmly.

"Well I suppose I could let him out on bail," muttered Mark, as he reluctantly unlocked the garden shed. A scruffy boy emerged, blinking into the afternoon sun. Mark handed him a dog-eared envelope and held out a notepad and pen. "Prisoners property – sign here." Geoff stuck the envelope under his arm and scribbled on the pad.

"See you tomorrow!" said Geoff cheerfully. He ran up the garden and disappeared through the kitchen door.

"Mark!" his mother's voice drifted out of the door again. "Your Dad will be down for dinner soon. He is working nights tonight. Now go and wash up for dinner."

"But I've got a lot of paperwork to do, Mum!" said Mark.

"You can attend to that after dinner. Don't hold your dad up. Now go wash your hands," she replied.

"Can I go to work with you tonight Dad?" asked Mark, over dinner. He regularly requested this and was occasionally rewarded with a trip to the police station.

"No Son – I need you to stay home and look after your mum." There was a note of tension in his dad's voice.

"Can we visit the station later?" begged Mark.

"Not tonight, I won't be there," he said.

"Where will you be Dad?" Mark was intrigued.

"I've got to deal with some very bad people tonight, Son," he replied.

"You are very brave Dad," pronounced Mark. "Is bravery the most important thing to be a good policeman?"

His dad thought for a moment and then said very slowly and thoughtfully, "Mark, it takes many qualities to be a good policeman and bravery is just one of them. The most important quality is integrity. You must also have compassion, empathy, self-discipline, a desire to preserve life, protect the vulnerable – and a sense of humour!"

"What are compassion and empathy Dad?" asked Mark.

"It means you have to care about people, Son," he replied with a gentle smile.

"I must be off," said Mark's dad, rising from the table. He kissed his wife and held her just a little longer than usual, reluctant to let her go. Then he crouched, hugged Mark and placed his police helmet on Mark's head for a moment. "You are in charge of security," he said to him with a smile, then took his helmet back and placed it on his own head. He stood at the long mirror in the hallway a moment, checking his uniform. Beside him, Mark straightened his own costume police uniform. His dad gave Mark's hair an affectionate ruffle before smoothing it and saying, "I think we are both fit to report for duty." With that, he opened the front door and went out to work.

*

Mark was woken by the sound of a knock at the front door. His mum passed his bedroom door on her way to go down and answer the door.

"Stay in bed Mark," she said, trying to get him to go back sleep, but Mark detected a frightened note in her voice. By the time she had reached the front door, Mark was sat in his dressing gown at the top of the stairs. He could see blue flashing lights through the window above the door.

Mark's mother opened the door. Two senior police officers in smart uniform with a lot of silver braid were standing there.

"May we come in Mrs Vardy?" one of them asked.

She opened the door to them, her heart pounding and her face contorted with apprehension. She already knew why they were here and knew what would happen next – although she desperately wished she was wrong in her fears. They took their hats off and came in. She showed them to the living room and closed the door behind them, leaving Mark alone. A familiar face appeared in the open front doorway. It was Mark's father's best friend and colleague, Sergeant Yeald. He gave him a look that said a thousand things yet nothing at the same time, before disappearing into the front room after his mother and the top brass.

Sergeant Yeald emerged a few minutes later and made his way up the stairs to Mark. He sat on the top of the stairs with him.

"What's happening? Why is the Commissioner here?" asked Mark.

"I spoke to your father earlier Mark," said the Sergeant. "He told me he had left you in charge of security and looking after your mother."

"Yes Sergeant."

"Well, something terrible has happened and you are going to have to be very brave and strong dear boy. Do you think you can do that?"

Mark blinked back tears, knowing what he would say next.

"I'll try."

*

Days passed by in a blur. Mark's mother was constantly crying; a procession of friends visited and drank tea with her in the little kitchen. No one talked to Mark about what happened. He felt helpless; he couldn't console his mum, and he was also unwilling to face his own feelings.

He remembered his father's words: "You are in charge of security."

Mark decided that the best thing to do would be to open his police station in the garden again. He made a series of minor arrests and the neighbourhood children were locked in his shed for suitable periods of time. Each evening, a different neighbouring mother knocked at the door to bail their children out for tea time. Each morning, Mark went to the real police station and made his report to Sergeant Yeald.

"Officer Vardy, come to deliver my crime report for yesterday," Mark announced. "I arrested Geoff Jones again for cycling without any lights on a pavement. I arrested Peter Dixon for scrumping apples in Farmer Giles's orchard. I arrested Lily Wilson for fighting with Zeb Wilson and causing a breach of the peace. They all served time in my jail and were released on bail."

"Three arrests in one day, dear boy?" said Sergeant Yeald. "I wish all my officers could match your arrest rate. You are a chip off the old block. Your father would be proud of you. How's your mother doing?"

"She is still crying all the time Sergeant. We have to go up to London tomorrow to receive dad's award."

"I know. Well, pass on my regards to her and tell her I will see her tomorrow for your dad's presentation"

*

The next day, Mark and his mother were up early and on the train platform to catch the train to London. Waiting for them there was Sergeant Yeald. He greeted Mark's mother with a hug, received a salute from Mark, and they all got on the train together. Mark had never gone further than the next stop on the train before, so he watched avidly out the window as the train made its way into the capital. As the factories, housing blocks and various buildings flitted past, Mark wondered who lived and worked in all these places.

When they got to London, they took an underground train to the Embankment. This was very exciting. Mark was amazed at the really tall flights of stairs and escalators that took them deep underground to the maze of tunnels and platforms below. He found it a little scary to think that the train was taking them underneath the big City of London. He was particularly concerned at the idea of a train going under the river. He wondered aloud whether the river ever leaked into the tunnels.

12

Sergeant Yeald assured him it was quite safe.

When they emerged from the underground, up yet more escalators and stairs, he was excited to see lots of famous buildings and landmarks. To his right was Big Ben, Parliament, Westminster Abbey and Westminster Bridge. They turned left onto the Embankment and walked alongside the River Thames. He could see a large domed building on the other side of the Thames.

"What's that?" asked Mark.

Sergeant Yeald replied, "That's St Paul's cathedral. It looks beautiful when it is all lit up at night. You should see it."

Mark hoped he would one day, perhaps when he was all grown up and a police officer in London.

They walked a little further and then sat down on a bench to eat sandwiches, the river in front of them and the Scotland Yard building behind. After polishing off a sandwich, Mark hopped up, wanting to look at the Scotland Yard building. This was the centre of all his dreams and ambitions; this is where police officers came from. He had seen the building in police dramas on the television; it was like a character in its own right. This was where his father was to be honoured.

He looked up at the imposing building. A figure stood at a window on the second floor. Mark couldn't make out any more than an outline, but he wondered who it was and whether they were a very important police officer. He wondered whether he would stand at that window one day.

The presentation passed like a surreal dream. The Police Commissioner who had come to the house that terrible night made a fine speech about Mark's father and presented his mother with the Police Gallantry medal that had been awarded to his father posthumously.

On the way home, Mark sat staring at his father's medal in its velvet-lined box. Very little was said. Everyone was deep in thought. Mark's mother's eyes were shining with both pride and grief. She looked at Mark, thinking for a moment about what the future may hold for him. She wished she could keep him home and safe forever, but knew that was not possible. He had his own adventures to live.

*\* Five years later \**

There was an almighty crash as twelve-year-old Mark shoved his prisoner through the swing doors of the police station. Holding him with one arm behind his back and another to his neck, he marched him up to the front desk. Sergeant Yeald raised an eyebrow.

"Yes, Mark? What do we have here, dear boy?" Sergeant Yeald had the well-spoken voice and expressions of an old soldier.

Mark enthusiastically nodded to one of the Wanted posters on the wall. "I got him, Sergeant! He's wanted on suspicion of burglary."

His prisoner, a spotty youth of around fourteen, did indeed match the poster. Sergeant Yeald didn't know whether to be pleased that they had their suspect or alarmed that Mark was now taking on more serious cases.

"Thank you, Mark, we will take it from here," he said.

Mark reluctantly handed his prisoner over to a custody officer.

"Can I take him down to the cells?" he asked hopefully.

"No lad – run along now," was the disappointing reply.

As Mark left the police station and trotted off down the road home, Sergeant Yeald picked up the phone and dialled a number. "Yeald here. It is time."

*

A few days later, when Mark sat down to breakfast with his Mum, there was a flutter from the letterbox. Mrs Vardy rose from the table and fetched the mail. She returned holding an unusual envelope. It was made of thick white paper and edged in silver. The address on the front had been written with an elegant fountain pen hand in dark green ink. It was addressed to 'Master Mark Vardy.' His mother handed it to him, with interest.

Mark was excited. No one wrote to him – not like this. He had never received such a special looking letter before. He opened it extremely carefully, keen not to damage the envelope. He pulled out the letter inside – again, it was on expensive-looking, thick white paper, edged with silver and written in cursive dark green ink. He read the letter carefully, looked confused, tried again and then handed it to his mother.

"I don't understand," he said.

Mrs Vardy took the letter and read it out. "Dear Mark, Congratulations! You have been awarded a place on the summer selection course for The Academy. Please find enclosed details." She looked at him. "Well it seems pretty clear to me, dear," she said. "You are being invited to their selection course".

"But I didn't apply!" said Mark. "What is The Academy?"

Mark's mother smiled. "It is the college that your father studied at before he joined the police force. It is a very special place and only very lucky young people are invited to study there. It's not a place anyone can apply to join. Instead, they are scouted by alumni from the college. Someone must have spotted you and recommended you."

"Who could that have been?" pondered Mark.

"I doubt you would have to look much further than Sergeant Yeald," his mum said with a smile.

"That would mean...Sergeant Yeald went there too!" exclaimed Mark.

"How else do you think he became your father's best friend?" asked Mrs Vardy.

"What do they teach there?" said Mark. "I want to be a police officer"

"The Academy trains young people to have extraordinary skills. Some become police officers. Some become soldiers. Some follow other paths. But if you want to become a police officer, this school will make you a very special, elite kind of police officer. That's what your father was."

"Then I shall go," Mark decided. "I will go and pack".

"Well, you aren't due there until next week." His mum laughed.

"A warrior is always prepared," said Mark with a grin and rushed upstairs.

## Chapter 2

Mark sat by the window and looked out of the train as it sped on its way. His mother had put him on the train at London, with his suitcase and brown paper bag containing his sandwiches and a bottle of juice. His mother was very keen on furnishing people with sandwiches and this epic journey called for his very favourite sandwiches – chocolate spread and banana.

*All great adventures start with a journey*, thought Mark.

As he looked out of the window, his mind was a jumble of many things. Mainly he was very excited. He was on his way to becoming a police officer; this was all he had ever wanted. He had dreamt of this for as long as he could remember. He would become like his father – a hero and a protector. He remembered his father's words to him, "Protect your mother." Although he didn't want to leave his mother, he knew that the only way he could protect her was by training and learning — becoming what he needed to be.

The city scenes in the window gradually became interspersed with the countryside as the London suburbs gave way to towns, villages and the fields in between. He had eaten his sandwiches by the time the train arrived at a big city by the sea. The train headed along the coast and Mark was fascinated to see the docks with their very tall cranes.

The scenery soon changed; he saw forest and heathland. Mark

18

looked out in amazement. He had never seen anything like this. Where he had grown up, there had been the moor, but he had never seen a forest. He started counting trees but gave up very quickly. There were more trees than he had ever imagined being in one place.

There was an announcement from the train guard that the next stop would be his stop. Mark's ears pricked up. He gathered his suitcase, put his sandwich bag in the little bin between the seats and wrestled the suitcase down the aisle towards the door. When the train door opened, he pulled his case out onto the platform of an old-fashioned railway station. A tall, slender man in a smart black suit, with a black shirt but no tie, was clearly waiting for him. He approached Mark immediately.

"Master Mark Vardy?" he checked.

Mark nodded "Yes, sir".

Mark had been brought up to address adults with respect. He thought it might be a very good idea to treat this man with respect. There was something very still and dangerous-looking about him, even though he had only been polite and pleasant in his manner so far.

The tall man introduced himself. "I am from The Academy. I am here to collect you."With that, he took Mark's suitcase very easily, as if it weighed no more than a small bag of carrots. "Follow," he said briefly and walked rapidly away. Mark followed him up a flight of stairs, over a bridge and down the other stairs. Waiting outside was a big, sleek black limousine. The man put Mark's case in the boot and opened the door for the boy. "Your carriage awaits," he said with a half-smile.

Mark's jaw dropped. He had seen cars like this in films, but not in real life. He could not believe that he was being asked to get into this incredible looking car. He didn't need to be asked twice though and scrambled in, babbling questions about it.

"What kind of car is this? Is it yours? How big is the engine? Is it a police car?"

The man ignored the questions and simply said, "It's not a long journey. You will soon be at The Academy."

Mark did as he was told. As the car took him on his way, he didn't know whether to look at the car's amazing interior or out the window at the scenes that unfolded. He saw a small village, with pubs, shops and a church. They drove through a ford at the bottom of the high street, and he exclaimed with excitement as plumes of water flew up on either side of the car. Then they were in the forest. There was heathland, and so many trees. His eyes flew wide open when he saw ponies just wandering around without any people.

"Are those wild horses?" asked Mark.

"Pretty much," answered the driver "They all belong to people called Commoners, but they get to run wild out here and live a fairly natural life".

"What are *they*?" asked Mark as they passed some very large animals with long shaggy orange coats and long twisting horns.

"They are Highland Cattle," was the reply.

"And they are wild too?"

"Pretty much," came the reply again. Clearly the driver didn't find this subject as interesting or surprising as Mark did. Mark wondered what sort of magical place he had come to where there was a forest and wild animals like this.

Before long, the limousine slowed, before stopping in front of tall, wrought iron gates. He pressed a button in the car and the gates smoothly sailed open, revealing a long straight drive, lined in Lime trees. At the very end of the drive was a glimpse of a magnificent building: a beautiful country manor house. Mark's mouth and eyes widened in disbelief. He was so amazed that he had no questions, which was unusual for him.

The car glided up the drive and stopped at the foot of a set of stone steps. The driver got out and came round to the door and opened it. Mark peered around as he climbed out of the car, and looked up at the building ahead of him.

"It's a mansion!" he exclaimed.

The building was indeed a substantial one, with great wings stretching left and right and tall turrets pointing up. It was several stories high and had beautiful windows that shimmered with diamond shapes in the light. A massive ornately carved

21

wooden door opened and a smartly dressed butler appeared.

"Good afternoon Master Vardy. Please come in." He stood back and gestured through the open door. Mark turned to retrieve his suitcase. The car had already gone.

"Don't worry about that," said the butler. "It will be taken up for you. I expect you are hungry after your journey. Would you follow me to the refectory please, young man?"

## Chapter 3

Mark followed the butler through a tall wooden door in the entrance hallway. It opened into a large hall with two long tables running the length of it, with benches either side. At the far end of the hall was a slightly raised platform on which there was another table that filled the width of the hall. This was clearly the High Table, where the teachers sat.

The room was a mixture of grey stone and dark wood. Tall windows flooded the room with light through diamond panes that cast shimmering rainbows on the walls and glittered off a range of mounted weapons. Everything about this room spoke of history and quality. Mark was impressed. He wondered whether his mother would allow him to put some words on the wall in their dining room at home.

Sat at the nearest end of the long tables were about twenty other boys and girls of around Mark's age. They were tucking into piles of sandwiches, crisps, cakes and fruit and drinking juice from crystal glasses poured from large crystal jugs. Each jug held different coloured juice. One of the boys looked up at Mark; he had a very friendly face.

"Hello! I'm Charlie. Why don't you sit with us? The food is brilliant."

Mark turned to look up at the butler for permission, but he was already gone. Mark wondered how he had disappeared without

23

him noticing. But his manners overrode his curiosity, and he smiled back at Charlie and extended his hand.

"Mark Vardy. I'm going to be a police officer," he said.

Charlie grinned. "Me too!"

He shuffled along the bench to make room for Mark. Mark sat down and helped himself to food from the large platters on the table. Although his mother had packed him his favourite sandwiches and it hadn't actually been that long ago that he had eaten them, he was already hungry again. He decided that any place that greeted him with lots of nice food must be a good place to be.

More boys and girls gradually arrived in the hall and joined them. They were all a bit muted and overawed by their surroundings and sat and ate politely.

"These must be all the students on the selection course," said Charlie. "Do you think we will all get selected?"

"I don't know," said Mark. "But I hope we are!"

"I'm sure I will be," said a pretty, golden-haired girl sitting opposite them. "My name's Pandora."

"Why do you think you will be selected?" asked Charlie with friendly curiosity.

"Because I'm good at everything and everyone loves me,"

Pandora pouted. "And I will sulk if they don't choose me. No one likes it when I sulk."

Mark looked at her incredulously. He had never known anyone so spoiled. Charlie giggled. Before he could say more, a quiet, elegant-looking Chinese girl slipped in quietly and took a seat. She made a little bow to her companions at the table before putting a little food on her plate and pouring a glass of juice.

"Hello, I am Mark and this is Charlie and Pandora," Mark introduced everyone to the new girl. The girl gave a shy smile

"I am Lucy," she said, "My mother and grandmother work here and I live here but this time I am allowed on the selection course." She looked down and fidgeted with her hands in her lap.

"What's up?" asked Charlie.

Lucy gave a sad smile "If I don't pass the selection course, I have to go away to an ordinary boarding school. I don't want to leave here."

There was a loud sound as the butler re-appeared and hit a large gong. All the children fell quiet, turned and looked. Standing at the head of the tables was a tall, older man in a smart suit.

"Good afternoon," he said. "I am Professor Ballard, the principal of this Academy. I would like to welcome you all here today. I hope you enjoyed your snacks and left enough room for dinner tonight?" He smiled and there were a few students who grinned back at him.

"This is the beginning of a great opportunity for you. For some, it is the beginning of a great journey too. As you see, many have been invited." He paused. "Though, few will be chosen." Another pause.

"This is a competitive course. We only accept the very best to join our Academy. We are looking for very specific qualities. At this stage, most of you will not even understand what these qualities are or why we value them. So you must try your best in every way. We want to see what you can do, what you can learn, and we want to see who you are."

The students looked at each other. Some looked nervous. Some looked competitive. A couple looked almost smug because they were quite sure that they were what the Academy was looking for.

The Professor continued. "Over the next few weeks, you will be taught the basics of martial arts; you will experience the foundation of what it's like to be a warrior. You will be tested and observed. However, you may be asked to leave at any time. You may choose to withdraw from the selection process at any time. Even if you reach the end of this course without voluntary withdrawal or being asked to leave, there is no guarantee that you will be selected."

He paused again. "But if you are selected, you will receive a full scholarship to the Academy and you will have the opportunity to train at this school for at least the next five years. All your costs will be covered, so this would be at no cost to your family. All you will need to do is study, train and become the best you can be."

A sea of eager faces looked up at him, excited now.

He smiled. "Now, run along. Settle into your rooms and explore the grounds for a couple of hours. Then wash your hands and report back here for dinner at six o'clock."

## Chapter 4

As the Professor left, two older students appeared. They were about sixteen, a boy and a girl. Both wore sharp black martial arts training suits. The girl had her black hair tied back in a sleek ponytail. The boy had short spiky hair, shaved close at the sides.

They both made small bows."Ladies! Please come with me" said the girl. "Gentlemen, with me please," said the boy. They set off out of the dining hall and the students scrambled to follow as they led them out of the dining room, up the grand flight of stairs in the hallway and further stairs to an upper floor. Then the girls were led to a corridor on the left and the boys to a corridor on the right.

"These will be your rooms whilst you are here. Each room is for two students. You can settle into your rooms and then you can explore the grounds outside." The girl with the shiny ponytail walked along the corridor, calling out names and gesturing to the rooms. Pandora pushed ahead of her new roommate into the room and assessed it quickly before sitting down on one of the beds. "I'm having this one." It wasn't clear why she preferred it but she had clearly decided it was the better of the two. Both the beds were exactly the same – immaculately sheeted in crisp white cotton. Her new roommate made no objection and sat down on the bed on the right. She was a pretty looking girl with a gentle smile and curling brown hair. "Hello, my name is Nell," she said. Pandora looked her up and down, again making her assessment. She decided that Nell would make a temporary companion who might prove useful. "I'm Pandora," she said, "Shall we go and explore?"

In the boys' corridor, the boys were being shown their rooms too. Mark and Charlie were pleased to find that they would be sharing a room. Mark thought Charlie was a fun, friendly sort of boy who he could share adventures with. "Let's go and see what's outside!" said Charlie. Mark agreed and they met up with many of the other students as they all made their way back down all the stairs, into the grand hallway and out the front door.

The older students were waiting for them. "You can walk around with us or explore on your own," they said. Most of the students joined this little tour group and then gradually wandered away as they found things to explore.

The grounds were extensive and beautiful. There were large expanses of beautifully level grass, old mature trees, hedgerows hiding secret areas, beautiful large flower beds bursting with flowers of all shapes and colours. Behind the main house, there were other buildings. The tour guide students explained as they walked past at a respectful distance "Some of these buildings contain staff quarters. Don't get caught messing around here. They don't like it.". They led their group down a winding path to a large building and opened the doors. "This is the Summer Dojo," said the older boy. "This is where your lessons will be".

The students peeked inside the Summer Dojo. It looked like it was from another country. Inside, the floor was covered in thick beige matting. The walls were lined with racks of weapons and equipment. At one end was a large chair with a picture of a wise-looking old Japanese man hung above it. "Who is that?" asked Mark. "That's O Sensei," said the older student. "He was the originator of Aikido. We revere him. You will too one day - if you are lucky enough to receive his training handed down to you."

Mark looked again at the picture, wide-eyed wonder on his face. His mind was racing with questions and curiosity. Before he could ask any more, the older students were ushering the students out, closing the tall doors behind them and leading them off up the track again. The track came to a junction. The path ahead led off towards a gate that entered into the forest. But they followed the track to the left and curved around behind the Summer Dojo and towards a new set of buildings. "This is the stable yard," said the older girl. "We are taught about horses as part of our training. We are taught to ride..." she smiled and paused "and many other things!".

The stable yard was immaculate – a square of large loose boxes from which a few horse heads stuck out to look at the visitors. A wide gap at the far end of the square opened up towards green pathways that led to paddocks lined with post and rail fencing. The fields swept up a hill and there were swathes of trees and forest at the top of the field under which a herd of horses sheltered from the afternoon sun.

The ponytailed girl and spiky-haired boy did not linger here. Before the students could flood into the yard to look more closely, they swept them on and around the grounds, pointing out areas of interest. They took them to an area that looked like an assault course. There were all sorts of obstacles made of wood and rope. Mark thought this looked like a lot of fun and was exactly what he had been expecting at this place.

Finally, they arrived back at the entrance to the main building. "Now go and amuse yourself and be back for dinner in an hour," said the older girl and then left them. Mark, Charlie, Pandora and Lucy drifted together, as they had met earlier in the dining hall. They wandered around, chatting and exploring. "I have lived here all my life," said Lucy. "I can show you the herb garden if you would like?". Without waiting for a reply, she led the way to a wooden door almost hidden in a stone wall. Behind the door was a walled garden with lots of flower beds. In each bed there grew a different type of herb. Lucy walked around, stroking the herbs and giving the names of each. "How do you know all that?" asked Charlie "You must be really clever". "My Mum is the doctor here and my grandmother was before her. All the women in our family are healers."

Mark and Charlie looked impressed. Pandora turned her nose up and said "Well I don't see the point in that. Herbs are silly. And we are here to become ninjas, not doctors." With that, she walked off out of the garden. The others followed, looking a bit embarrassed that Pandora had been so rude to Lucy. "Well, I think it sounds jolly useful and important," said Mark to Lucy, supportively. Lucy gave him a grateful smile. She had felt hurt by Pandora's comments.

As they made their way out of the garden and down the path, they saw a man in the distance pushing a wheelbarrow. A horse walked along beside him and the horse and the man seemed engrossed in conversation. At first, it looked like a reasonable sight to see in a place like this where there were gardens and horses. But there was something a bit unusual about it. Mark was instantly fascinated. He liked unusual things and interesting people. He hurried forward, with Charlie and Lucy. "Who is he I wonder? Let's go and say hello," he said. Pandora stopped, put her hands on her hips and said "Why do you want to talk to him? He's just a gardener."

Mark was getting a bit fed up with Pandora and her rudeness. "But what else is he?" asked Mark. "My Dad told me that no one is just anything. Everyone is many things and most of them are interesting in some way. There is something special about every person you meet."

Pandora huffed "Well he doesn't look interesting to me. You do what you like. I am going to find something interesting to do."

## Chapter 5

Mark, Charlie and Lucy hurried off after the gardener. "Excuse me, Sir," said Mark as they drew closer, a little out of breath from running after him. The gardener stopped, turned and smiled at them. "Hello Lucy," he said, "Have you brought some friends to meet me?"

"Yes, Mr Liu," she said "This is Mark and Charlie. They are going to become police officers." "And ninjas!" chimed in Charlie with a big grin.

"Is that your horse?" asked Mark, looking up at the big brown horse who stood at Mr Liu's side and regarded him with equal curiosity. "She is my companion and partner," said Mr Liu. He turned to the horse "TigerLily, I would like you to meet young Mark here" he gestured to Mark and the horse stretched out her nose and sniffed him. Satisfied, she looked at Mr Liu. "And Charlie" he gestured again and once again the horse stretched her nose out and this time sniffed Charlie's hair before whiffling it with her lips. He giggled. "And of course you know Lucy," said Mr Liu to the horse. Lucy stepped forward and smoothed the satin coat on TigerLily's neck.

For a moment all this seemed normal. Then a slightly confused look appeared on Mark's face. He had just been introduced to a horse. He didn't know a lot about horses but something seemed unusual here. "Do you love gardens?" he asked the boys. "This one is jolly neat Sir," said Mark. "But do you love it?" asked Mr Liu. "You have to love something to truly appreciate it." Mark

33

put his head on one side, thinking about his reply. Finally, he settled on "I don't really know it, Mr Liu". "Well that's the wisest thing you could have said," said Mr Liu. "You must love to appreciate and you must know to love. So we must start with your getting to know."

"Thank you, Sir, but I have come here to learn to be a police officer and a warrior like my Father. I don't think there will be time for gardening." Mr Liu smiled "There must always be time for gardening, even if that just means spending time appreciating it. Tell me, have you ever done The Noticing?" Mark and Charlie shook their heads. "What's The Noticing?" they asked. Lucy smiled – she knew all about this. Mr Liu looked at Lucy "Tell them about The Noticing Lucy". She answered, "The Noticing is when you walk around a garden and notice everything that has changed, everything that has grown, everything that has died, the little creatures that live in the garden, the new buds, the freshly opened flowers, all the new growth."

"Why would you do that?" asked Mark. Mr Liu answered "A garden is a system in flux and growth at all times. Every day is different and each member of the garden is different every day. But the garden grows and changes at a speed you can keep up with. Plants will never grow faster than you can walk. So you can take your time, really see everything around you and decide if you need to do something. That's a bit like being a warrior, isn't it?"

"But it sounds awfully slow," said Mark. "Warriors are fast". "That's a matter of perception," said Mr Liu. "You must master the very slow before you can master the very fast. Time isn't what you think it is. If you are to become a great warrior, you must learn about time. You cannot control what you don't understand."

As he said this, he began wandering along a flower bed, touching the flowers, pulling off flower heads that had died, cutting back bits of foliage. His horse walked alongside him, nibbling at the grass. "It's a lovely day, isn't it?" he said to TigerLily. She looked up a moment. He stroked her neck and then she dropped her head down and carried on eating grass.

"Why do you talk to your horse?" asked Charlie curiously. "It would be a bit strange to have a friend and not talk to them, wouldn't it?" said Mr Liu. " I talk to her to find out what she is thinking and feeling. But it isn't all words. There are different ways to talk with horses."

"What are they?" asked Charlie. "It's a big subject and there is too much to tell before your dinner time," said Mr Liu.

"I think I would like to learn some gardening Sir," said Mark "and how to talk to horses".

"Come another day and I will tell you some more. You had better go back to the house for dinner now though."

"Goodbye, Mr Liu," they all said and headed back towards the house. Mark looked over his shoulder. The big brown horse was watching him intently. "Goodbye TigerLily" he called back. Mr Liu smiled and turned to TigerLily and whispered something to

35

her.

## Chapter 6

The students crowded through the dining room door just in time
for dinner. Place settings had been set at the long tables. The
butler appeared and ushered them to their seats. When all were
seated, he tapped the large gong and this signalled some waiters
to appear and deliver bowls of steaming soup and baskets of
warm freshly made bread.

Having spent their afternoon exploring, the students were all
hungry and tucked into their food immediately. "Ugh! What's
this?" asked Pandora. A waiter quietly replied "Carrot and
Coriander Soup Miss". "I don't like it. It's weird" she said.
Actually she rather liked it, but she wasn't going to admit it.

"Well I think it is delicious," said Mark. Charlie giggled "I think
you say that about a lot of food!". Mark grinned "I do! I am
always hungry and I always like everything I am given. My
Mum says I am easy to feed." he paused "Do you think there are
some people who are hard to feed?". Charlie nodded towards
Pandora and they both giggled.

After the soup came the main meal. Bamboo covered baskets
filled with rice were brought and all sorts of dishes were passed
around the table from which the students helped themselves to
various vegetables and bean curd in different tasty sauces. There
was bean curd in lemongrass and garlic which had a lovely
delicate flavour. There was aubergine in a slightly spicy and
salty brown sauce. There was steamed broccoli and carrots.
There was cauliflower in a gentle curry sauce. There were dishes

37

with cashew nuts, with bamboo shoots and bean sprouts. The food was every colour and flavour of the rainbow. The students tried everything, carefully exploring at first and then piling their plates with food as they realised how tasty and delicious it all was.

At the end of the meal, the waiters appeared and cleared the plates. Then they reappeared with individual silver bowls containing different coloured ice-cream which they set before each diner. The students were full from eating so much, but no one could refuse ice-cream! "What flavour is it tonight?" asked Lucy. The butler smiled "There is coconut milk ice-cream with caramel ripples. There is almond milk ice-cream with peanut butter swirls and chocolate chunks. And there is cashew nut ice-cream with chocolate sauce."

"The ice-cream isn't made of milk?" questioned Mark.

The butler nodded "No one died for your dinner young man. You will find that we are very keen on not hurting others at this Academy".

Mark was too polite to enquire further, but he found all this surprising and hard to understand. When the butler had once again disappeared, Charlie said "I thought the whole point of martial arts was to hurt people. So why are they worrying about animals? And not wanting to hurt anyone?"

"My Dad said that a good police officer must care for people," said Mark. "Perhaps this is something to do with that. Perhaps we have to care for animals too."

Pandora made another rude sounding noise. "I don't care about anyone and I certainly don't care about animals. I just care about winning a place at this Academy and I am going to do it."

The others exchanged looks with each other. They were beginning to find Pandora's attitude a bit hard to cope with.

After dessert, warm herbal tea was served in small round bowls. "To help you sleep," said the butler. Mark and Charlie looked at the tea suspiciously. "It's just herbs" whispered Lucy "We drink it every night. It won't hurt you. It just helps your digestion and relaxes you for bedtime."

The students stayed chatting whilst they drank their tea. Another crash on the gong came when the butler informed them that it was time to go up to bed now.

"You have a big day ahead of you tomorrow ladies and gentlemen. Breakfast is at eight in the morning. Your training clothes have been provided in your rooms. You must report to the Summer Dojo wearing these at nine o'clock. I advise you not to be late. But for now, sleep well"

The students went up to their rooms. Laid out at the end of their beds was a pile of neatly folded white clothing with a belt on top. They climbed into their beds and whispered excitedly to each other.

"I wonder what will happen tomorrow?" said Nell.

"I am going to show everyone what I can do," said Pandora. "If we are meeting in the Summer Dojo, it must be for martial arts. I have been going to Karate school for two years, so I am really good."

Nell had had just about enough of Pandora by now. "Night night," she said, then turned out the bedside light between them, rolled over and made it very clear she was going to sleep. Pandora had been expecting to talk about her Karate knowledge for longer, so was a bit put out. She huffed again and noisily turned her back on Nell. "What a rude girl!" she thought.

## Chapter 7

After breakfast, the students arrived at the Summer Dojo. Most
of them had arrived early and were lined up outside. Mark and
Charlie were at the head of the line having rushed in their
eagerness to get to their first lesson. They were all wearing the
white training suits that had been laid out for them in their rooms
and had attempted to tie their belts in various ways. Pandora was
missing, but by ten to nine, everyone else was there.

At nine o'clock precisely, the doors of the Summer Dojo opened
and a new figure stood there – a tall, well-built man with sandy
coloured hair. He wore a similar suit to the students, but it was
black and tied with a black belt with nine silver stripes on the
end. He looked at them a moment and then stood back and
gestured them in, indicating that they should line up along the
edge of the dojo. Inside already were the two senior students
who had been their guides yesterday.

The students had fallen silent. They were a bit intimidated by
this man and awestruck by the large and impressive dojo. He
walked along the line of students, taking a moment to look at
each of them. They felt like he could see right through them.
Charlie giggled nervously when it was his turn at the head of the
line. The man stopped, paused a moment and then said "Why are
you laughing? You haven't heard any of my jokes yet!". He
laughed and all the students relaxed a bit and laughed with him.

"Now, let me introduce myself. My name is Heath Goodwin.
You can call me Mr Goodwin. If and when you think I have

taught you something useful, you can call me Sensei Goodwin."

"You have met my assistants, Bella and John, already. They are here to help me help you."

"First things first, let get you all dressed properly. That white suit you are wearing is called a Judogi and there is a particular way you should tie your belt. Everyone gets it wrong at first and I see you lot are no different!"

He gestured his assistants towards the students "Sort them out!"

As the assistants went along the line, teaching the students to tie their belt, the door was thrown open and in marched Pandora.

"Nice of you to join us," said the teacher.

Pandora looked at the other students being taught to tie their belts. "Oh it's okay, I know that stuff," she said airily.

"We are very lucky to have such an expert amongst us," said the teacher. There was a note in his voice that implied that he may not be very impressed but Pandora was oblivious so she smiled and looked pleased with herself.

The teacher returned to the class. "Let's start with a few basics. We are going to learn to stand like a martial artist and move like a martial artist. Those feet are for moving, not sticking to the ground. So let's get them moving."

He proceeded to demonstrate, pointing out how they should stand, with their legs shoulder-width apart, one behind the other, one pointing forwards and one pointing slightly to the side. He told them they must get their hands up, so they are ready to defend their head. Then he taught them how to move, shuffling the leading leg in the direction they were moving and slightly dragging the other behind so that their feet never crossed or stepped past each other.

"Your turn!" he said. "I want you to stand properly and then shuffle halfway across the Dojo and then shuffle backwards to where you started. Go!"

The line of students started shuffling across the Dojo. Some tripped themselves up, some bounced along on their toes, some got muddled and had to start again.

He smiled "You will get it. Practise that every day until it is as natural to you as breathing. You do all breathe, don't you?" he joked. There were giggles from the students.

"Next we need to teach you not to get hit. It's pretty important to not get hit. Getting hit can really ruin your day. So I think you should all become experts at Not Getting Hit."

He called the older student, John forward "Give me some punches, nice and slow so they can see what we are doing". John gave him a steady volley of slow punches from a range of angles. Sensei Goodwin easily stepped outside the punches, deflected them or stepped inside them, blocked them and returned a tap to the boy's chest to show that he could have punched him if he needed to. He stopped, thanked John and addressed the class "So you see. However the punch comes, I am going to evade it or

43

block it. Let's start you with some simple window wiper blocks."
He turned to John who then gave him a series of slow
roundhouse and uppercut punches. He swung his fists round at
the Sensei's head, left and right, then punched upwards from his
hip to the Sensei's chin, again on the left and right. Sensei stayed
still but swung his arms up one at a time to block the roundhouse
punches that were coming to the side of his head. Then he swung
his arms down to block the uppercut punches that were coming
to his chin.

"Do you think you can do that?" he said "Have a go – but be
very careful not to actually hit each other. You are here to train,
not to hurt anyone. I will joke about a lot of things but I am
completely serious about this. Do not hurt each other. Go as slow
and carefully as you need to in order to stay safe. Now get into
pairs and try this – carefully! I don't want to have to send any of
you to the doctor."

The students got into pairs. Mark paired up with Charlie and they
started doing what they had seen demonstrated. They really
enjoyed it. It was like a real fight but very slow and careful. But
they didn't mind. It was really fun!

At the other end of the Dojo, Pandora had paired up with her
roommate, Nell. It wasn't long before there was a thud and Nell
was on the floor with her nose bleeding. Pandora stood there
looking a bit irritated that the girl was making such a fuss.
"That's your fault. You should have blocked better" she said.

"Stop!" Sensei's voice rang out. He went to Nell, checked her
and then asked Bella the assistant to take her to the doctor. Then

he turned to Pandora. "How long have you been here?" he asked with ominous politeness. Pandora, as usual, was oblivious to the undertone. "This is my first day, but I have been doing Karate for two years!" she said boastfully.

"Well, I am sure that's not how your instructor taught you to treat your training partners. You have been here less than one day in fact and you have hurt someone already."

He paused "Leave my mat".

Pandora looked incredulously at him. He pointed to the door. Pandora opened her mouth to speak and thought better of it. She turned, huffed and stalked out.

He faced the class once again. "I hope we all learned something today"

"Yes Sensei" they all replied. He smiled "Now carry on practising"

## Chapter 8

Whilst the rest of the students went to lunch, Pandora had found herself summoned to Professor Ballard's office. She was very sulky having been sent out of the martial arts class. Didn't that instructor realise how good she was? She knocked on his office door. "Come" came a voice from within. She opened the door and went in.

The office was panelled in dark wood which matched the large desk at which he sat. He gestured to a seat facing him and Pandora sat down, a disgruntled expression still covering her face. He thumbed through a folder then set it down and addressed her. "Miss Black. I regret to inform you that you have not come up to the standard required for this Academy and your time on this selection course is over."

Pandora's jaw dropped with amazement. Surely there was some mistake? "What?" she said. "Why?!"

"Your attitude has not been what we would expect in one of our students. You have been arrogant and rude, both to students and our staff. But worst of all, you have struck and hurt another student through carelessness and showing off and then showed no care, compassion or concern for her. There are many things we can teach you Miss Black, but we cannot give you a good character nor instil in you compassion for others. We have the highest standards here at the Academy and you have not met them. So it is with regret that I must send you away. A car will be waiting for you outside to take you home in half an hour. I suggest you go and pack your case."

Pandora still looked at him with amazement. "But you invited me here!"

He looked at her seriously. "Actually, we had wanted your sister, Xinia. But when we spoke with your mother about inviting her, she asked us to take you instead. She felt that Xinia is a good girl who will do well wherever she goes. But she felt that you were more in need of this opportunity. Normally I would not have considered such a swap. But your mother has been of great service to this Academy and our country. I cannot refuse her anything within my power. So I agreed, against my better judgement."

Pandora was looking furious now. "You wanted Xinia?" she practically spat her sisters name out. "You should have wanted me. I am much better. She is a goody goody. She is always off playing with her horse but she doesn't do anything with it. She doesn't even do competitions. I am brilliant at karate and I have won rosettes for show jumping."

The Professor was running out of patience. "We look forward to meeting her. I have phoned your mother and explained our decision to send you home. And we have offered your place on the selection course to Xinia, who I am glad to say will be joining us in the morning. Good day, Miss Black."

Pandora glared at him and said as threateningly as a twelve-year-old girl can "You'll regret this!"

47

"Even so" he replied and turned his attention back to paperwork on his desk.

Pandora stormed up to her room and ran into some of the other students who had finished lunch and were going back to their rooms to change for their afternoon lesson.

Two of the students were chatting excitedly. "It's Ninja Skills this afternoon". "I wonder what that will involve," said the other. "I don't know but it sounds brilliant!"

Pandora pouted. She knew she would have been really good at Ninja Skills. She hurried to her room and packed quickly, throwing everything into her case and stuffing it in. Then she slammed the bedroom door and dragged the case down the stairs.

Outside, the big black limousine was waiting for her. The driver put her case in the boot and opened the door for her. She looked back at the building. There was no one there to wave her off. She narrowed her eyes. They would all regret this. They would all be sorry. This wasn't over.

## Chapter 9

The students met outside the Summer Dojo, as instructed. They were very excited to be going on a Ninja Skills training session. They were clad in Judogis, but instead of the white Judogis they had worn for Martial Arts training, these Judogis were a green and brown camouflage print. On their feet, they wore black trainers with thick rubber soles with strong grips designed for off-road running and climbing.

They were chattering excitedly amongst themselves when three shapes suddenly emerged from the forest nearby. They had been standing there watching the students for some time but had been hidden amongst the trees by the camouflage Judogis and stillness.

Two of the figures the students recognised – it was Bella and John, the older students. Between them stood a very neat looking Japanese man. His eyes gleamed as he looked at them. "Welcome to Ninja Skills! I am Sensei Kochi Tanaka. You may call me Sensei or Sensei Tanaka. You have met my assistants already."

"Our lesson today will be out in the forest. We are going to learn to navigate in the forest." He led them down the path, through the gate and into the open forest beyond.

"Now, is everyone ready? Then follow me!" with that he slipped away into the forest. The students hurried after him. They got about twenty foot into the forest and realised they had lost him.

"Where's he gone?" asked Charlie. Mark scouted around but couldn't see him. "I can't believe we have lost him already," said Mark. "He can't have gone far. We had better wait."

Sensei Tanaka stepped out from behind a tree. He grinned "I thought I told you to follow me?!". The students laughed, but it was as much from relief as sharing the humour. "Lesson one!" said Sensei Tanaka "Never take your eyes off your target. Let's go!".

He set off at quite a pace, leading them through trees, along narrow paths, across ditches and over trees. After a few minutes, he stopped. "Which way is home?" he said.

The students looked around. Most pointed back down the track. Mark pointed away at an angle. Some pointed in all sorts of wrong directions.

Sensei Tanaka smiled at Mark "Very good! What's your name?".

"Mark Sir – I mean Sensei," said Mark.

"Lesson Two!" said Sensei Tanaka "Always know the direction of home!". He paused "The path is not always straight. In fact, it is not very often straight. You must learn to develop an internal compass so that you always know the direction of home. The way can change, but the direction does not."

He set off again, talking as he went "Pay attention to the landmarks! Every plant and tree is a landmark. A river is a landmark. And where there are no clear landmarks in the landscape you can make your own Waymarks." He stopped, gathered 3 pebbles and laid them in a triangle at the base of a tall oak tree. "So!" he said "Waymark!". Then he walked on a little further, gathered some sticks and made a little cone sticking up from the undergrowth. "Waymark!" he said.

He stopped by a big fallen tree with shaggy plants tumbling from it. "Look!" he said, "Can you see the big shaggy monster in the shape of that tree?". The students stared at it, some putting their heads on one side as if that would help them see better. "Try and see characters in the trees. It will help you remember them."

"Can't we just carve the trees?" asked a big dark-haired boy called Bob. Sensei Tanaka looked very seriously at him. "First, I hope you have not been so wicked as to bring a knife to this Academy! And second, I hope you would not be so wicked as to harm a tree! Goodness! Whatever gave you such an idea?!" Sensei Tanaka walked off making tutting noises.

The walk continued until they came to the river. "Cross the river!" said Sensei Tanaka. The students looked into it. It was shallow, but they would get very wet if they walked through it. Some of them started towards climbing down into the river. "No!" said Sensei Tanaka. "I don't want to take you home wearing the river!" He led them along the river bank a little to where there was a big tree that had fallen over it. "Like this!" he said and nimbly scampered over the tree to the other side of the river. "I said to cross the river, not walk through it. Is there anyone here from London?" he asked. A few hands went up. "If

51

I told you to cross the Thames, would you try and walk through it?"

"No Sensei!" they said.

"There are many ways to cross a river. Bridges are good ways!" he chuckled.

The students all followed him over the fallen tree to the other side of the river, some struggling to balance and others confident and agile. One or two looked a bit nervous but they tried anyway and very soon everyone was on the other river bank. Sensei Tanaka led them further into the forest, stopping to make a Waymark here and there and encouraging them to do so too.

Suddenly he stopped. "Now I hope you have all been paying attention and spotting landmarks and making your Waymarks. I want you to turn around and lead us all home." The line of students turned back to face the way they had come and headed off back down the path. Mark and Charlie had been at the head of the line and now were at the back on the way home. Suddenly they realised that Sensei Tanaka and the older students were no longer with them. "Sensei?" called Mark. The other students looked round. No one could see Sensei Tanaka. "He's left us!" exclaimed Nell. "How are we going to remember the way home?" asked another.

"Sensei wants us to find our own way home," said Lucy "That's the lesson". "We had better find our Waymarks," said Mark, taking the lead. He started looking and soon found a cone of sticks. "This way!". The students picked their way back through the forest, everyone looking out for landmarks and Waymarks. There were cries of "Found one!" and "This way!". They were soon back at the river they had crossed. Mark led the way across and Charlie helped the students climb onto the log to cross, offering them a hand up. Then they resumed their search for Waymarks "Let's stick together! We don't want to lose anyone" called Mark.

As they made their way back, a silent figure watched them from behind trees. Mark thought he saw someone a couple of times but thought he must be mistaken.

When they made it back to the Summer Dojo, Sensei Tanaka appeared behind them. They wondered how long he had been there. Lucy smiled. She suspected he had been there all the time.

Sensei Tanaka clapped his hands. "Very good! I am glad you all found the way home. Tomorrow – another lesson. Now you may rest and play in the grounds until dinner"

## Chapter 10

Over dinner, the students were excited after a day of Martial Arts and Ninja Skills. "Which bit did you like best?" Charlie asked Mark. "I liked it all!" said Mark. "It was all brilliant. I can't wait for tomorrow!"

"I liked the Ninja Skills best," said Charlie. "It was all good though," said Lucy "I wonder what they will teach us tomorrow?"

The dining-room door opened and the butler showed a new girl in. She was a slim girl with long brown hair and serious eyes. The butler showed her over to the table where Mark, Charlie, Lucy and Nell were sitting "This is Miss Xinia Black" he said, "I hope you will look after her and make her welcome". Xinia gave a shy smile. Lucy and Nell shuffled apart on the long benches of the dining room to make room for her. She gratefully took a seat between them.

The students introduced themselves to her then Nell said "Are you related to Pandora Black? She was here but she went away yesterday". Xinia sighed "I'm her sister. But I am nothing like her. People say we are like chalk and cheese. I hear Pandora got thrown off the course?". "She punched Nell," said Lucy seriously. "That sounds about right. Are you okay Nell?" asked Xinia. "She made my nose bleed, but I am okay now thank you," said Nell.

"I hope we can be friends," said Xinia "I am sorry my sister hurt you." Nell smiled "Of course! And I think we shall be roommates too!"

During dinner, the butler tapped on Bob's shoulder as he sat at the next table. "You are to report to Professor Ballard's office after dinner". Bob ate his dinner up quickly and then went to the Professor's office as directed. He knocked on the door and opened it when the voice from within said: "Come".

The Professor was standing at his window looking out. He gestured to the seat in front of his desk and Bob sat down. The Professor continued to look out, leaving a long and awkward silence during which Bob looked around. To his horror, he saw that his folding knife was laying on Professor Ballard's desk. He took a sharp intake of breath.

Professor Ballard turned and looked at him. "Yours I believe?". Bob considered denying it a moment but realised it would be pointless. "Yes," he said, hanging his head.

"When did you last remember having this knife?" asked the Professor.

"Out in the forest Sir," said Bob.

"And yet it is here now," said the Professor. "That tells me that someone took this off you." he paused "And you didn't even notice!".

"Yes Sir," said Bob miserably.

"There are many reasons why we tell students not to bring knives to the Academy. And there are many reasons why you should not carry one outside in the world. You have just learned one of them. If you carry a knife, that knife can be taken from you and it can be used against you. You are lucky that you learned this lesson without getting hurt. Today someone has taken your knife from you, without you even knowing, and now it is laying on the desk before you. If you do this out in the world, the next time you see your knife may be when someone stabs you with it."

"It is a shame you will not be staying here long enough to learn the other reasons why it is unwise to carry a knife. But if you have learned nothing else from your short time here, I truly hope you have learned this lesson. I cannot allow you to stay after breaking such a serious rule. I am sure you will understand this."

"Yes Sir" mumbled Bob, trying not to cry.

"Now go and pack. The car will be waiting for you outside in half an hour."

## Chapter 11

The next morning, the students had their second Martial Arts class with Sensei Goodwin.

"Good morning!" he greeted them with enthusiasm. "Yesterday we started on the very important subject of Not Getting Hit" He emphasized the last three words. "You learned how to block incoming punches with your arms. Now we are going to learn how to Not Get Hit without laying a finger on our opponent. Doesn't that sound fun?"

The students all nodded keenly and wondered how they could avoid getting hit without touching anyone.

"In fact, we aren't going to use our hands for this at all. We are going to use our feet!" Sensei Goodwin continued. "Does anyone know how we can do this?"

Charlie's hand shot up "Are we going to kick them Sensei?!" he asked.

Sensei Goodwin laughed "Well that would be one way and sometimes that might be the best thing to do. But I want to show you a much more gentle way. I am going to avoid getting hit, using my feet – but not touch my opponent."

He gestured to his assistant, the spiky-haired senior student. "Now, I would like you to give me a series of straight punches, please. Nice and slow so they can see what we are doing."

The assistant aimed a punch at Sensei Goodwin's nose. Sensei Goodwin simply stepped to the side and turned his body sideways so that the punch went straight past him but made no contact. Then he stepped back in front of the student who delivered a punch with his other hand. Again, Sensei Goodwin stepped to the other side this time and turned his body sideways. He watched the punch fly into the thin air that he had previously been occupying.

He turned to the class and grinned. "Got it?!" They all nodded. "Have a go then! And go nice and slowly. The point of this is to learn and practise footwork, not to hit each other."

The students attempted the exercise. Sometimes they turned the wrong way or forgot to turn at all. Sometimes they forgot to move at all. Sensei Goodwin went round the class, correcting anyone having difficulty. Very soon they had all got the hang of it and were executing neat little steps and turning their body out of the way of the punch, as they had seen Sensei Goodwin do. He was pleased.

The practise went on for a while and then they repeated the shuffling and blocking they had learned the day before. Some bore this with greater patience than others.

He clapped his hands and the class lined up along the edge of the Dojo. "Who here has ever built a house?" he asked them. The students looked confused.

"No one?" he laughed "Well if you ever do build a house, you will have to build foundations for that house first. Without foundations, your house would crumble and fall. Martial Arts is like building a house in this way. You must build foundations. "

He walked up and down the line, still talking "Footwork is one of the most important foundations. If you can't move in a safe and effective way, you will fall over. If you can't step out of the way of an attack, you will get hit. If you can't block a punch, that punch will hit you and hurt you."

He stopped his walk and turned and faced the students before saying seriously "Martial Arts involves practising things many times. If you are not prepared to do this, you should walk away now. There are no shortcuts to excellence. Everyone has to do this. Only those with the patience and self-discipline to practise will succeed. Does anyone want to quit?"

The students all shook their heads. Sensei Goodwin smiled. "Excellent! Then you have all taken a step along the path to becoming black belts. A black belt is a white belt who never quit. You have not quit today. Keep not quitting and you will discover what you can become. Have you thought about what that might be yet?" he looked at them with a challenge in his eyes. Their eyes widened at the thought.

"You have done well this morning. So this afternoon, we are going to go on a little field trip. Wear your Ninja Skills judogis and trainers. Now go and get some lunch – but I suggest you make it a small lunch!" he chuckled and bowed to the class as they bowed in return.

## Chapter 12

After lunch, the students turned up outside the Summer Dojo and were surprised to see a black minibus waiting for them, driven by the driver who had picked many of them up from the railway station. He opened the sliding door for them and cried "All aboard!".

The students clambered into the minibus and they set off on a drive that took them through the forest, through the countryside and then to a place they had not seen before. It looked like a quarry of some sort. The bus stopped and they got out. Waiting for them was Sensei Goodwin who greeted them "Good afternoon. I hope you enjoyed your lunch. Now stand here please and watch. This is very important – do not move!"

He walked away from them and stood with his back to the base of a tall wall of chalky rock. Facing him was a steep slope. Sensei Goodwin looked up the slope and raised his hand. The students followed his gaze to the top of the slope. Up at the top were Sensei Tanaka, the Ninja Skills instructor, and the two senior students. In front of them was a large rocky boulder.

Sensei Goodwin dropped his raised arm. This was clearly a signal to the team at the top of the slope because one of them removed a chuck from in front of the boulder and then they all pressed down on a plank that was wedged under the back edge of the boulder. The students gasped in horror. The boulder started rolling down the slope, gathering speed dramatically. They looked at Sensei Goodwin, terrified that the boulder would roll down and hit him. It was so big and heavy and moving so fast, it must surely kill him! Some of the students screamed.

At the very last moment, Sensei Goodwin simply stepped out of the way of the boulder and turned his body sideways – exactly as they had seen him do in the Dojo that morning. He lightly tapped the back of the boulder as it passed him and then crashed into the wall of chalky rock.

The students heaved a big sigh of relief. He walked over to them and smiled "Now do you see the value of footwork?". "Yes!" they all cried.

"Now that was a big demonstration and it could have gone very badly wrong if I had made a mistake. Do you know how many times I have practised that footwork?"

The students shook their heads. "Neither do I – but it would be many tens and even hundreds of thousands of times. And it was still dangerous. So don't do this at home!"

He grinned "But you can do the footwork at home. In fact, you will practise that footwork every day. I think you will understand a little better why it is necessary in future."

"Now, it's your turn to do something interesting. I do hope you heeded my advice about a light lunch. Climb up that slope and report to Sensei Tanaka."

The students scrambled up the slope together to where Sensei Tanaka was waiting at the top.

"Important Ninja Skill! You must learn to descend on a rope!"

With that, he hopped over the edge of the cliff edge with a black rope wrapped around his body and descended elegantly to the ground below. The students looked over the edge and watched him. "Wow!" said Mark and Charlie "I want to try!".

Mark and Charlie were first to volunteer to make the descent. Sensei Tanaka and the two senior students helped them to prepare, giving them gloves and helmets, securing their safety harness and line and showing them how to feed the rope so that they would descend under control. They went down easily and gave a cheer when they made it to the bottom.

The students followed, two at a time. Some found it easier than others, but all had made the descent until there were just two students left. Billy and Nell had hung back, not wanting to volunteer to go next. Neither wanted to do this.

Sensei Tanaka turned to them and asked "Ready?". Both Billy and Nell shook their heads. Sensei Tanaka started with Nell. "What's wrong?" he said. "I am frightened Sensei," said Nell miserably. "What's there to be frightened of up here?" he asked. She looked a bit confused by his question. "Well, nothing Sensei. I am scared of going over the edge".

Sensei Tanaka smiled "Well if there is nothing to be scared of up here - no lions or tigers - then you shouldn't feel scared yet. Do you agree?". Nell nodded. She could see his logic. "Now take a deep breath and think about how safe you are up here. There is nothing to worry about."

Nell did as he said. She took a really big breath, held it and then let it slowly out, looking around her. He was right. There were no lions or tigers here.

"Now then, let's get you kitted up," he said "and remember, there is nothing scary about the safety equipment. There is nothing to worry about yet." he smiled at her and held his hand out to give her confidence. She took it and allowed the older students to kit her out.

"Focus on the gloves as you put them on." said Sensei Tanaka "They won't hurt you, there is nothing to worry about". Nell agreed. The gloves felt nice and were soft inside. They put a helmet on her head and fastened the strap under her chin "The helmet isn't anything to worry about either" smiled Sensei Tanaka "and this is your safety harness and safety line." He checked all the equipment for her, as he had for all the previous students. "We only use the best of equipment. Your equipment will not let you down. Sometimes people let the equipment down - but it will never let you down!" he laughed.

He guided her to the edge and explained how she should feed the rope. "You will not lose control. The safety device will mean that you can never just slip down the rope. So there is nothing to worry about, is there?". Nell nodded.

"Now I want you to promise me that you won't worry about anything until it is time to worry," said Sensei Tanaka. "Can you do that?". Nell nodded again "Yes Sensei".

"Now let the rope out a little and go down two feet," he said. Nell did as she was told. "There is nothing to worry about yet is there?". "No Sensei," she said. "And again - go down two feet please," he said. Nell obeyed again. "And another," he said. "There isn't anything to worry about yet is there?". "No Sensei" she called up.

Two feet at a time, Sensei Tanaka talked Nell down the drop to the ground below. As her feet touched down on the ground, the other students cheered. They knew how hard this had been for her. "Nell!" called Sensei Tanaka. She looked up "Is there anything to worry about yet?". "No Sensei!" she called back, laughing.

Sensei Tanaka turned to Billy, a tall, strong-looking boy with messy brown hair. "So you see," he said, "Nothing to worry about."

Billy backed away from him, fear in his eyes. "Now Billy - what is there to worry about up here? No Lions! No Tigers!"

"I can't do it Sensei," said Billy. "How do you know if you don't try?" asked Sensei Tanaka. "I just can't," said Billy.

Sensei Tanaka turned and fetched a helmet and gloves. "Do you think you could put these on?" he said. "Well yes," said Billy "But I can't go over the edge.".

Sensei Tanaka smiled calmly "I am not asking you to go over the edge. I am asking if you can put this helmet and gloves on."

"Okay," said Billy "I can do that. But I can't do anything else"

Billy put the helmet and gloves on. He didn't see the point, but he obeyed.

"Now, can we put the safety harness and line on you?" said Sensei Tanaka. "That can't hurt you, can it?"

Billy agreed - the harness wouldn't hurt him. He allowed it to be put on.

"Now come to the edge," said Sensei Tanaka. Billy tried. He stepped close and looked over.

"No! Oh goodness No! I can't do it Sensei!" he said. His pulse was racing and he heard it pounding in his head. He started backing away from the edge, panicking wildly.

"There is nothing to worry about," said Sensei Tanaka. "No one is going to push you. You will only step over that edge if you want to. You have all the safety equipment you need. You can do this in your own time. But I don't want you to be scared until there is something to be scared of."

Billy stopped backing and stood there breathing heavily. "I am scared now Sensei!" he said.

"What are you scared of?" asked Sensei Tanaka

"I am scared of falling," said Billy

"Well that doesn't make sense," said Sensei Tanaka. "You have seen how the equipment works. You will only descend at the rate you feed the rope through. You have a safety line, a helmet and gloves. You can't fall and you are very unlikely to hurt yourself if you are sensible."

"Will you try it?" he said

Billy could see his logic, but there was something in him that just could not accept the logic and not be afraid. He moved slowly to the edge and looked over. The ground seemed to rush up to meet him. It loomed ominously. He felt sick.

Billy pulled away again. He sat down, shaking. "I'm sorry Sensei. I just can't. I want to go home."

Sensei Tanaka knew real fear when he saw it. This poor boy had a phobia of heights. He had given him the opportunity and tried to help him overcome the fear, but some fears were very hard to overcome. He patted the boy on the shoulder. "You tried," he said. "This is not for everyone."

As they were getting on the bus, Mark looked up at the cliff edge they had been abseiling down. For a split second, he saw a figure standing there – all dressed in white and wearing a white ninja mask. He blinked. Surely he was imaging it? When he looked again, the figure was gone. "Did you see someone up there?" he asked Charlie. Charlie had been too busy chatting with the other students. He shook his head. "It must have been Sensei Tanaka Mark". But Mark could see Sensei Tanaka talking with Sensei Goodwin and the senior students nearby. This figure had been someone else, someone unaccounted for. He wondered who it was and why they were watching.

On the bus on the way home, Billy was subdued. His fellow students were kind to him about what had happened, but he knew he had failed. He knew his time was up and there was no point staying on the selection course. They would not choose him and he couldn't see the point in staying and having to face his fear of heights again.

When they returned to the Academy, he went straight to the

Professor's office to withdraw from the course. The Professor was very gentle and understanding with him. "Never mind young man. This path was not your path. But there is another path out there waiting for you. Go out into the world and seek it."

## Chapter 13

Over dinner, the students talked excitedly about their day. "You were awfully brave Nell," said Lucy "I know you were scared". "But you did it!" said Mark "That was great!"

"How did you find it Xinia?" asked Charlie. Xinia smiled "I enjoyed it thank you". Charlie decided that Xinia seemed a lot more polite and nice than her sister.

"Who is the man with the horse?" asked Xinia "I saw them on the grounds when I arrived yesterday".

"That's Mr Liu," said Lucy "and his horse is TigerLily. She is very clever. She follows Mr Liu everywhere!"

"I would love to meet them," said Xinia "I really love horses and I am going to miss my horse whilst I am here."

"We can take you to meet Mr Liu and TigerLily after dinner if you like," said Lucy. "Yes please!" replied Xinia, her face lighting up. She had only been at The Academy twenty-four hours now but she was pining for her horse already. She worried about whether he would be sad without her, whether they were looking after him back home and giving him enough cuddles and treats.

Xinia ate her dinner up impatiently. She had a feeling the aching sensation in her chest would soften if she could just hug a horse. She looked pleadingly at Lucy and the others. They grinned and finished off their ice cream quickly.

"Come on then," said Lucy and she, Xinia, Mark and Charlie got down from the table and went off in search of Mr Liu. They found him in the rose garden again. He smiled as they approached "Ah – my little ninjas!" he said, "How was your day?".

"It was brilliant!" said Mark. "This is Xinia. We said we would bring her to meet you because she really likes horses."

"Is that true?" Mr Liu asked Xinia.

"Oh yes Sir!" she said "I have a horse of my own and he is the best person in the whole world! I really love him and I am missing him already." Xinia looked a little sad.

"What's his name?" asked Mr Liu

"Rainbow" replied Xinia, a smile softening her mouth as she said his name. She couldn't help but smile when she mentioned him.

"Why is he called Rainbow?" asked Mr Liu.

"Because when the light shines on him and you look just the right way across his coat, you can see millions of tiny rainbows," Xinia replied

Mr Liu looked at Xinia with great interest. "You must look very closely at your horse. Not many people look that closely. It is quite...unusual" he said with a thoughtful pause.

Xinia continued "But when he feels different things, the colours change sometimes. When he is excited, the rainbows are blue. And when he is upset, the rainbows are red."

"And when he is really happy?" asked Mr Liu

"The rainbows are gold" replied Xinia with a dreamy smile on her face as she remembered such times.

Mr Liu looked at her with great interest. "You are Anna Black's daughter, aren't you?" he asked.

Xinia nodded "Yes Sir"

Mr Liu smiled and had a faraway look in his eyes as if remembering a distant memory. "She was an extraordinary horsewoman too."

Mr Liu seemed to suddenly shake himself back into the present. "Where are my manners? Xinia, I would like to introduce you to TigerLily." He turned to his horse "TigerLily, this is Xinia".

TigerLily took a small step forward and sniffed the back of the hand that Xinia offered. Xinia was dying to reach forward and hug her, but she knew that would be rude. They had only just been introduced. She nodded her head down slowly until it was close to TigerLily's. "You are beautiful" she whispered to her. TigerLily responded by closing the gap until her head was next to Xinia's and they were eye to eye. Both Xinia and TigerLily took a long, slow breath together. "So beautiful" whispered Xinia again and placed her hand softly on TigerLily's jaw. They stood together a few minutes and it seemed the world had shrunk to a small bubble that just contained the pair of them.

Mr Liu watched and did not interrupt or interfere. He knew that TigerLily would only allow what she was happy with and he knew that Xinia was in no danger. But he was very interested to see how this girl related to horses and how TigerLily responded to her. She had potential, a lot of potential. He could see she was undoubtedly her mother's daughter and had inherited her gift.

Mr Liu signalled to the other children to leave Xinia with the horse and return to the school. He returned his attention to pruning the roses, leaving Xinia and TigerLily sharing a special moment.

After a while, TigerLily exhaled then backed away. Then she turned and followed Mr Liu. Xinia watched her go. The pain in her chest had gone and her head felt full of a warm, golden glow. "Thank you" she breathed quietly after TigerLily.

**Chapter 14**

The following morning, the students turned up at the Summer Dojo for their Martial Arts lesson. But instead of the friendly Sensei Goodwin, there was a new instructor waiting for them there. He was a younger man, not as old as Sensei Goodwin. He was tall, with long black hair and a moustache. He looked like a Muskateer, but scarier and clad in a black Judogi with a strange pair of trousers that looked halfway between trousers and a skirt. No one dared ask him if he was wearing a skirt. In fact, no-one dared ask him anything. His expression was intensely serious and there was an air of distinct darkness about him.

The students lined up along the edge of the Dojo. He bowed and they bowed quickly in return, eager to show their newly acquired Dojo manners. He didn't bother to introduce himself as the other instructors had. Instead, he pointed to Mark at the head of the line and gestured him forward onto the mat. Mark obeyed and as he was doing so, the instructor went to the wall and lifted down a long wooden sword. He returned to Mark and held the sword high above his head. "Evade!" he said sharply and brought the sword down. Mark stepped smartly out of the way and turned his body to the side, in just the way that Sensei Goodwin had taught them. "Good," said the instructor. "Return".

Mark went back to the line. "Next!" said the instructor sharply, looking at Charlie. Charlie stepped out to where Mark had been. "Evade!" The wooden sword came down and he too nipped to the side and turned his body. "Good!" said the instructor.

74

"Next!"

He worked down the line and every student had their turn evading the wooden sword. It was quite alarming and a good test of the skill they had learned. When he had finished and every student had been tested, Mark thought he saw a shift in the shadows at the door of the Dojo. The door was open. He thought it had been closed. He wondered whether someone had been watching. Perhaps it was the mystery ninja he had seen at the chalk quarry and in the forest?

The instructor returned the wooden sword to the mounting on the wall and instead chose a long sword in a scabbard. He drew the sword from the scabbard and raised it high. The sun glinted off it.

The students gasped and stepped back. Surely he didn't intend to test them with this too?!

"Any volunteers?" he asked, an extremely dangerous glint in his eyes. The students practically flattened themselves to the wall of the Dojo in their attempt to withdraw from him – all except Mark who stepped forward. "I would like to try Sensei!" said Mark. "Then step onto the mat young man," said the instructor, watching him closely.

Mark took up the same position he had taken before – just in front of the Sensei. He looked up at the gleaming sword and made a mental note that it would be very important to evade this sword when it came down. All the students gasped. Mark's focus became extremely sharp. All that existed in his world at this moment was the sword and himself.

The Sensei replaced the sword in the scabbard at his side. He almost smiled at Mark. Mark suspected that this was a man who did not smile very much. "Return!" he said.

Mark returned to the line. He was half relieved that he had not had to evade the sword and half disappointed that he didn't get the chance.

The Sensei pulled a black silk scarf from his jacket and threw it in the air. It was so light it hung there a moment before drifting downwards. In a dramatic flash of silver, the Sensei had drawn his sword and flashed it through the silk. The scarf fell in 2 pieces to the floor.

"This is a Samurai sword. It is sharper than a razor blade."

"If this had cut you, it would have killed you," he said to Mark. "There are some things you can try but there are some things you can only do. Never try to do the things that simply must be done. You must learn the difference."

"A hunter can make many mistakes. The prey can only make one."

"Until you can evade with such skill that you will never fail, you cannot face the blade of a Samurai Sword. This is a lesson. Don't just practise until you get something right. You must practise until you cannot get it wrong. Next time you ask for this test, be sure this is the case."

"You were brave," he said to Mark. "And foolish. But also brave."

He paused a moment and said in a low voice with a distinct tone of warning "However if you get any more confident, you will be dangerous."

He replaced the sword on its mount on the wall. "Now!" he said "I will teach you to fall and roll. This will be necessary for your martial arts training. If you cannot fall without hurting yourself, you will not be able to do very much training. So this is important."

With that, he taught the rest of the lesson on the subject of falling and rolling. He taught them to make their body curl up in a ball and just roll across the mat when they are thrown. He made them go across the mat in a series of forward rolls and then backwards rolls. He taught them to crouch, tuck their heads onto their chests and to curve their arms so they became part of the curve that led their body through rolls.

The students were quite exhausted by the end of the lesson. They had rolled over and over so many times they weren't sure they could stand up any more.

"Enough," he said with a clap of his hands.

He bowed, they bowed and he gestured to the door. The lesson was over and they filed out. They still did not know his name.

**Chapter 15**

Anna Black sighed as she dismounted from the big black police horse. It had felt like a long shift today, probably due to the hot British summer and busy crowds of London. She ran her stirrups up their leathers, lifted the saddle flap and loosened the girth to give a little relief to the gentle horse who had carried her so loyally today. Then she stroked his neck and whispered: "Thank you, Gabriel". She led him back to his stable and set about taking off his tack before removing her gloves and laying her hands on his back.

She massaged his back, her fingers rubbing small circles, lifting and smoothing his coat as she went. Her fingers sought out areas of tension in his muscles and rubbed them gently until they relaxed. Then she lay her palms flat on his back and rubbed with increasing pressure, restoring any circulation to the tissues of his back that may need it after wearing a saddle and carrying a rider all afternoon. Gabriel gave a long exhalation of breath and lowered his head, relaxing as she worked on him. Most riders didn't do this for the horse that carried them, but Anna was special. She knew how he felt and wanted to make him as happy and comfortable as possible.

When she had finished massaging him, Anna took up a brush and gradually worked over his coat, grooming him with care. As she was doing this, her fellow mounted police officer, Martin, appeared at the stable door. "How is Pandora doing at that special school you sent her to?"

"I'm afraid it didn't work out for Pandora, but Xinia took up her place there instead," said Anna.

"Where will Pandora go?" asked Jake.

"We're not sure yet" replied Anna. "It may have to be the local school. But I am not sure that would be best for Pandora. She needs.....more..." Anna trailed off, unable and unwilling to explain exactly how difficult Pandora is or why she might need a special school.

The following morning, there was a message waiting for her asking her to report to Superintendent

Michael's office before her shift. She wondered what he might want her for. She felt the faint urge to snarl. She really didn't like Superintendent Michael. There was something shifty and slimy about him. Nevertheless, she had no choice but to attend when summoned. So she went to his office and knocked on the door. "Come in!" he called, imperiously. His tone was one of a man who liked to sound as important as possible.

"Ah Anna," he said "How are you? How are things? Everything going well?" he asked

Anna didn't particularly want to discuss anything with him but politeness required a response. "Yes Sir. Everything is fine."

"I'll get straight to the point." Superintendent Michael said. "A little birdie told me that your daughter Pandora didn't get on at the Academy."

Anna looked at him in surprise. She hadn't discussed Pandora or her education with him in the past. She wasn't keen to discuss it with him now either. It didn't take her long to work out that it must have been Martin who had been gossiping about her. She would have some words to say to him later!

Superintendent Michael gave a creepy kind of smile that suggested he was quite pleased with himself. Anna felt her skin crawling with distaste for this man.

"I think I may be able to be of some assistance in this matter," he said. "The Academy is not the only special school for young martial artists. There is another which may turn out to suit young Pandora even better."

"Really?" asked Anna. She didn't want to take advice from this man, but she could not deny that she needed to find another school for Pandora and it was going to be hard to find one suitable because she was such a difficult girl.

"Oh yes," he said "It's a school for Ninjas. It takes young people and trains them to become elite operatives with a remarkably broad education and specialist abilities."

"I tell you what. Leave it with me. I have some contacts there. I will make some calls and see if they can do something for young Pandora."

"Thank you, Sir," said Anna politely. She may not like this man, but it sounded like he was going to be quite helpful to her on this occasion. She forced a slightly stiff smile.

## Chapter 16

The students were looking forward to an afternoon of Ninja Skills with Sensei Tanaka. "I wonder what we will learn today?" said Charlie with excitement.

"Perhaps another Ninja navigation walk?" wondered Mark.

He didn't have to wonder for long. Sensei Tanaka appeared from nowhere, as if by magic. He had a habit of doing that, Mark noticed.

"My little Ninjas!" said Sensei Tanaka. "Today we shall learn a new important Ninja skill! Follow me!". He set off down the path, through the gate and into the forest. The students hurried after him. No sooner had they got into the forest than he had disappeared. The students stopped and looked around.

"Where did he go?" asked Xinia. "I don't know!" replied Lucy "He can't be far away".

Sensei Tanaka stepped out from behind a tree. "Very close!" he laughed then continued "Today we start to learn the Ninja art of Stealth. Stealth contains many skills. It is the art of invisibility. It is the art of moving without detection. It is the art of disguise. It is the art of blending."

"Trees make excellent cover. Stand behind them and a person in front cannot see you. Stand very still and make no noise and they cannot hear you either. Everyone find a tree to hide behind!"

The students each selected a tree and pressed themselves close to it. "Excellent!" Sensei Tanaka said. "Now hold very still, slow your breathing right down. Don't make a noise! Press yourself to the tree. Blend with the tree. Become one with the tree. Become the tree!"

Sensei walked around. There were a few rustles of feet in leaves. If any student made a noise, he tapped them on the shoulder.

"If I tap your shoulder, it is because I heard or saw you. We will play this game a lot. You must learn to hide well and stay perfectly still and quiet. If I were a stranger walking through these woods, I should have no idea you are here!"

He clapped his hands twice. "Return!" he said and all the student slipped out from behind the trees. "Next lesson! Stealth Tracking! You must follow your target quietly and without being seen. This is a difficult skill. You must learn to pick your path carefully so you do not snap twigs or rustle leaves. You must stay in the shadows, taking cover behind trees. Do not allow your silhouette to appear on the horizon. If there is a light behind you and you are between that light and your target, your silhouette will show. Do not let this happen."

"Bella! John!" he called. The two senior students appeared at his side as if they had been there all along.

"Bella and John are going to take a walk through the forest. It is your job to Stealth Track them. If you make any mistakes, I will tap you on the shoulder and this means you have failed the task and must join Bella and John. Proceed!" he gestured to Bella and John to start their walk. Then he was gone.

The students all scurried away to their trees and hid behind them. Then they started following Bella and John through the forest. They did their best to move quietly and not be seen, but one by one they got a tap on the shoulder. Before long they were all tagging along behind Bella and John.

"Stop!" said Sensei Tanaka. "It's not so easy is it?" he asked them. They shook their heads and a few said "No Sensei".

"Well never mind. We will practise this a lot. You will soon become experts!" he laughed.

"Now, follow me, I have something else to teach you." Sensei Tanaka set off at his usual rapid pace.

He took them back through the forest and into the school grounds and then around the back of the house. They ended up in a garden. It was an oriental looking garden and had some large round boulders, an area of raked gravel and some colourful red and gold Acer trees.

"You see these boulders?" he asked. "Yes Sensei!" the students replied.

"I want you to curl up in a ball, with your arms folded around your head, and make yourself as much like one of these boulders as possible."

The students thought this a very curious direction but they all did their best. The knelt down, curled their bodies over and folded their arms around their head as he had told them to.

Sensei Tanaka smiled. "You may not make very convincing boulders during the day. But at night, when this garden is just shadows, you will be very effective boulders."

He wandered around, pleased with his boulders. "You must visualise being a boulder. Really concentrate and believe you are a boulder. Be still. Be a big rock. Be the boulder!"

Sensei Tanaka took a big breath and enjoyed his slow breath out. He smiled and then continued to walk around as the students remained curled up as boulders. "Practise makes perfect!" he said.

## Chapter 17

After Ninja Skills, they had an hour or so before dinner. The students made their way back to the school building, chatting amongst themselves.

"I'm glad that's finished!" said Charlie. "I thought I had turned into a boulder by the end of it!"

"I think that was the idea" laughed Mark. "Still, it could be a jolly useful skill. One day you might want to be a boulder!" They all giggled.

"We've got a bit of time before dinner, let's go see Mr Liu and TigerLily!" said Xinia.

"Oh yes, let's!" cried Lucy. Mark, Charlie and Nell agreed and they set off to find them. They found him at the bottom of the large lawn in front of the main building. A small river ran along the bottom edge of the lawn and disappeared under a bridge over which the main tree-lined gravel drive swept. Mr Liu appeared to be doing some form of exercise, but it was extremely slow. His arms and legs moved in slow motion as he moved through shapes and forms. He looked very peaceful. TigerLily grazed nearby under the trees. She raised her head as the students approached.

The children didn't want to disturb Mr Liu. They sensed it might be rude to do so. So they sat down under the trees and watched him quietly, wondering what he was doing.

After a while, Mr Liu came to a stop. He stood with his hands by his side, breathing slowly and deeply. Then he turned to the children and smiled at them. "Hello my friends!" he said.

"Hello Mr Liu!" they all said. Then Mark asked, "What were you doing Mr Liu?"

"What do you think I was doing?" he asked Mark.

"Well it was a bit like martial arts but a lot slower" replied Mark.

"Why do you think I might practise martial arts very slowly?" asked Mr Liu.

"So you can get it right?" guessed Mark.

Mr Liu laughed. "Well, you are sort of right. What I am doing is called Tai Chi. By moving very slowly, I can concentrate on exactly how I move my body. It makes me concentrate on my balance and how to keep my balance through all the movements. That's a lot harder to do when you move slowly, but if you don't have balance when you move slowly, you won't have it when you move quickly either. Slow is smooth and smooth is fast my friends!"

Lucy hesitated a moment and then said "Mr Liu..."

"Yes Lucy?" he encouraged her.

"I thought I saw something when you were doing that," said Lucy tentatively.

"What did you see?" Mr Liu asked Lucy.

Lucy screwed up her face, trying to find the right words to describe what she saw. "Sort of like lines. Lines made of light. They curved and streamed behind your hands and then there was a sort of glowing ball of gold light between your hands when they were close in front of you."

"You are a very lucky girl Lucy," said Mr Liu. "Someone can train all their life and not see what you have seen. It is a very special gift. You must use it well."

The other students looked at Lucy in amazement, except Xinia who had seen something too.

"You don't look surprised Xinia," said Mr Liu.

"I saw something too Mr Liu. I mean...I always see things....sort of glows around people, and animals. When you were doing that, I saw a bigger glow. I can still see it. It's bigger and it is still there."

Mr Liu smiled again "That is the other reason that I do this. To make my glow bigger. That glow is called Chi. It is also called Ki or Prana. Different cultures have different names for it."

"What is Chi?" asked Charlie, who was struggling to follow all this.

"It is energy, Charlie. It is life force. We all have it and the more we have, the healthier and stronger we are. Not just the kind of strength in your muscles, the strength of life force."

Mark liked the sound of that. "Would you teach us some Tai Chi please Mr Liu?!"

"It would be my honour young Mark". Mr Liu pressed his palm to his fist and made a small bow.

The students all spread out around Mr Liu. "We start by standing still, with slightly bent knees, our hands by our sides. And we breathe deeply, in and out," he said. The students did this. It was quite unfamiliar to them to think about breathing because normally it just happened naturally without them having to think about it, but they did their best and took deep breaths.

"Now copy me!" said Mr Liu. He stepped out with his left leg, placing the heel on the ground. Then he rocked forward onto that foot whilst sweeping his arms up together in front of him, his hands and wrists soft. Then he rocked back onto the heel again and let his hands point upwards so that his fingers seemed to paint the air like ten paintbrushes. Lucy gasped with excitement. She could see faint trails of light coming out of her fingers. Mr Liu smiled but continued. Then he took them through a series of movements, some of them strange and unfamiliar. Lucy's eyes were wide with amazement by the end of it. Xinia was also quite stunned by her experience. The boys looked very peaceful, which was unusual for them.

They all stood there, around Mr Liu, breathing deeply and very still. Then he turned and bowed to them again. Without thinking, they bowed back.

"Thank you Mr Liu!" they all said.

"How did you find it?" asked Mr Liu.

"That was great!" said Mark. "I felt like a Ninja but in slow motion. I felt really strong but also quiet and peaceful."

"Me too!" said Charlie "It was hard to keep my balance. I thought it would be easy because it was slow, but it was much harder!"

"It will become easy with practise," said Mr Liu "All things are easier with practise."

He looked at Lucy and Xinia, both of whom were quiet. "How about you two?" he asked.

Lucy spoke first "I saw a lot of strange things, Mr Liu. There were ribbons and balls of light, but they came out of my fingers and hands! And I feel sort of glowy. Is that a word? Glowy?"

"It's a very good word for what you feel," said Mr Liu "and you Xinia?"

Xinia was still looking stunned "I feel glowy too Mr Liu. And everything looks brighter. There are bright colours around everyone. More than usual. More than the usual outer glow that people have. It's like thousands of brightly coloured needles of light and they are dancing. Oh, I don't know. I can't really describe it. I feel connected to it all."

"Wow! I wish I saw that too" said Mark. "Maybe if I practise lots I will?"

Mr Liu turned to Mark "Maybe you will. Maybe you won't. Maybe you have other gifts. We are all different. But did you like how Tai Chi made you feel?"

"Very much so." said Mark "I could take on the world right now I feel so powerful". He flexed his arm muscles and everyone laughed.

**Chapter 18**

Pandora had a determined look on her face in the back of the car as her Mum and Dad drove her to her new school. At least there would be no silly selection process here. They had already accepted her and invited her to a short orientation course. Her place was certain though. She was going to the Shadowlands Ninja School!

Pandora had been expecting Shadowlands to be similar to The Academy and was looking forward to another beautiful mansion set amongst magnificent grounds. So she was more than a little shocked when they arrived at the school. It didn't look like a school at all. The approach road swept up to a stark wall of concrete, set forward from a long wall that clearly encircled the entire grounds. As their car drew up, a guard stepped out from behind the concrete wall. He was wearing camouflage uniform and carried a clipboard. "Pandora Black?" he asked.

Pandora stepped forwards and nodded. "Yes, I am Pandora Black. You can fetch my suitcase from the car."

The guard laughed. "I am a guard, not a footman. Take your own suitcase in."

Pandora's parents were surprised too. This place looked very stark and uninviting. They weren't too sure about leaving Pandora here. But they were clearly in the right place and Pandora was expected. Superintendent Michael had assured Anna that this was an excellent school for Pandora. So she nodded to her husband and he got Pandora's suitcase out. He

91

locked the car and both he and Anna went to follow Pandora in behind this strange concrete entrance. The guard stepped in front of them and said "I am sorry Sir and Madam. It is students only beyond this point."

"Oh!" said Anna "Well we had better say goodbye here then." She tried to give Pandora a big hug, but Pandora shrugged her off, ignored her father, grabbed her suitcase and marched off through the entrance. Her parents looked hurt, but they were rather used to being treated this way by Pandora.

"I hope we are doing the right thing," said Anna to her husband when they got back in the car. "I don't know what else we could do at this point" replied her husband grimly.

Pandora meanwhile had gone into the school grounds. It looked nothing like a school. All she could see were big concrete huts with curved roofs. There were no gardens at all. In the distance, she could see some sort of assault course. Pandora did not like the look of this place at all. But she was determined to stick it out and do better than her sister Xinia. This place might not be as posh and attractive, but if it turned out better ninjas, that was all she needed from it.

A student of about 16 stepped out of a nearby concrete hut. She was short, with black hair and mean-looking eyes. She looked Pandora up and down before saying "Pandora Black I presume?"

Pandora puffed herself up with her usual confidence and arrogance "Yes. I am Pandora. I am going to be the best ninja this school has ever seen. I have done two years of karate already and I can ride a pony!"

The girl laughed, somewhat unkindly. "Right," she said "Well we will see about that. First, you have to survive orientation."

"But I have been offered a place here!" said Pandora.

"That's as maybe," said the girl "But if you are too soft and ask to leave, that won't do you any good. So like I said, first you have to survive orientation."

The girl walked back towards the hut "Follow me" she said.

Pandora followed her, dragging her suitcase. The girl led her into the hut. Inside were a dozen beds, six on each side of the room. They were wooden and somewhat rough looking. Pandora looked horrified. "Do people sleep here?" she asked.

The girl laughed. "Oh yes. In fact, you will be sleeping here." She wandered down the line of beds to the end. Then she pointed to the bed on the right "That's yours."

Pandora's eyes flew wide open with shock. They could not possibly expect her to sleep here! She had never seen anything like it. She was expecting a pretty bedroom as she had at home. She turned to the girl who had shown her in but who was now walking away. "I can't sleep here," she said, "I won't be comfortable at all!"

"I really don't care," said the girl heartlessly and kept walking.

Not knowing what else to do, Pandora set her suitcase down and sat on her allocated bed. She sat there chewing her lip, considering her options. This was not what she was expecting and she didn't think she was going to like it here at all. But it was the only way to get back at Xinia and the only way she was going to get to become a ninja now. She decided to make the best of it.

## Chapter 19

After dinner, Mark and Charlie went to their room. It had been a great day and they were too excited to go to sleep. They stayed up chattering about what had happened and what they had done during the day.

"I love doing the Ninja Stealth!" said Charlie, "I think that's my favourite bit."

"I like the martial arts lesson best. It was so much fun doing the evading. I thought that Sensei was going to bring that sword down on me!" said Mark "I wish he had. One day I will be good enough and he will let me do the test."

"I bet you will! And it will be amazing!" said Charlie "I wonder what we will do tomorrow? I hope there will be more Ninja Stealth"

"I expect there will be" replied Mark "Perhaps we will have to become one with the trees again?" he laughed and pretended to be a tree. Charlie laughed too and pressed himself to the door. "I have become one with the door!" he giggled.

"Lights out!" came a call down the corridor outside.

The boys switched off the light, got into their beds and settled down to go to sleep. They slept well until the hoot of an owl outside woke Charlie. Charlie got up and went and looked out the window, trying to see the owl. Mark was woken by Charlie moving around in the room. "What's happening?" asked Mark sleepily.

"There's an owl!" said Charlie excitedly "It's outside, but I can't see it. Oh, I so want to see it! We don't have owls where I come from. But it sounded just like the owls in movies."

"Maybe if we go outside we will see it," said Mark.

"But aren't we meant to stay in our rooms until morning?" said Charlie.

"No one actually said that" replied Mark, who was very good at remembering rules and laws. "We wouldn't be breaking any rules. They just wouldn't expect us to do it. That's not the same thing as breaking rules."

Charlie had to agree but he was still a bit nervous about it. "What if we were to put on our Ninja Stealth kit and use stealth to get out without being seen?" suggested Mark.

"That's a brilliant idea!" said Charlie, brightening at the thought of playing stealth.

They both got dressed into their stealth gear and set off. They opened their bedroom door extremely slowly and carefully. It made a little squeak. They took a sharp intake of breath. But no footsteps came running. No one had heard.

They crept along the corridor, down the stairs and out the front door, which they were surprised to find unlocked. All the way, they moved slowly, quietly, pressing themselves against walls and moving very carefully so as to not make a sound.

Once outside, they hid against the building, waiting silently for the owl to hoot again. After a while, their patience was rewarded. "Twit Teroooo!" came the call. Mark spotted the outline of the owl on a branch of one of the trees that lined the driveway. He was dimly lit by the outside lights of the building. He pointed to him so Charlie could see. Charlie's mouth fell open. He was really amazed and very excited to see the owl. He wanted to say something, but couldn't because they were in stealth mode.

The two boys crouched and watched the owl for a while until the bird flew away, swooping silently down the driveway. Then they crept back inside the building. The door to the dining room where they had their dinner was on the left. On the right was another tall set of double doors. They had never been in there. Mark thought he saw a flicker of light from the keyhole. Curiosity got the better of him. Rather than go back to their room, he beckoned to Charlie and they slipped silently over to these doors on the right. Mark crouched down to look through the keyhole and Charlie kept an eye out for him to make sure they weren't caught.

Through the keyhole, Mark could see a large hall. In fact, it looked like another Dojo with charcoal coloured mats on the floor and swords on the wall. There was a flash of white. Someone was practising in there! He couldn't see very much through the keyhole, just a swirl of white robes and perhaps some long white hair? Whoever it was was almost flying around the room. There was a sudden flash as moonlight pouring through the window reflected off a glancing sword stroke. Then it seemed the swirls of robe, hair and sword seemed to leave trails of golden light behind them as they streamed around the room. Mark gasped. He had never seen anything like this.

Then suddenly there was another eye looking back at him through the keyhole. Mark jumped back in shock. He grabbed Charlie "Quick!" he hissed. They both flew back up the stairs to their room, as if a monster was after them.

"Wow – that was close!" said Charlie "What did you see?!"

Mark told him about the white ninja and the light streams. "Wow!" said Charlie "I wish I had seen that!"

"It was incredible," said Mark "But I hope we won't be in trouble. I don't think we were meant to see that."

## Chapter 20

Pandora was woken by a loud horn being blown in the rough dormitory she was sharing with 11 other girls. She opened her eyes blearily. The other girls were rushing around to get dressed and out the door. One of them shook her bedding as she passed "Hurry up sleepy! We have to be outside on parade in five minutes! Jump to it!"

Pandora scrambled out of bed and quickly changed into the camouflage combats and black boots she had been given the night before. She didn't have time to make her usually pretty long blonde honey-coloured hair look nice. She tied it back in a ponytail, put on the cap she had been given and rushed outside after the others.

The students were all lined up in two rows, organised by the girl who had shown Pandora to her bunk yesterday. Pandora joined the end of the line. The students now included a similar number of boys who had joined the group from another hut. An impatient looking man marched from behind a nearby building and stood in front of them, twitching irritably. He was middle-aged, although looked old to Pandora, had short-cropped hair and was very neatly turned out in his uniform. Like everyone else here, he wore camouflage combats.

He walked up and down the line, clearly not impressed with what he saw before him. "Right!" he said "Welcome to Shadowlands Ninja School. My name is Jack Adams. I will be your main instructor during this orientation course. You will call me Sir or Mr Adams. I am only Jack to my friends – and I don't have many of them. Ninjas don't have time for friends. Friends make you weak. If anyone here has any friends, I suggest you get rid of them immediately. Don't let others hold you back."

He continued his pacing "Whilst you are here, we will introduce you to what training at this school involves. You will walk. You will run. We will run you to exhaustion in fact. You will learn what your limits are and push beyond them. You will learn to climb, to swim, to hide, to track. You will learn the art of Ninja Stealth. And you will learn to fight."

"Who here considers themselves a nice person?" he asked in a tone that suggested that this might not be a good thing to admit to. None of the students dared put their hand up. "Good!" he said "We don't want any nice people. We want effective people, people who can learn, people who can do a job."

"The world out there is undisciplined, wild and ineffective. People of today think they can do whatever they like, say what they like, think what they like. You have come from this world. You are here to learn another way. You will become something different. And then you will go back into the world and make it different too. Do you understand?" he asked.

The students all nodded vaguely. They didn't understand but they didn't dare say so.

"Liars!! he screamed "You do not understand at all! But you will. And your lying will become one of your greatest assets as a ninja. Everything that the world calls a vice will become a skill for you as a ninja."

The students were completely lost. They had no idea what he was talking about but did not dare ask. They just stood still, a bit stunned and hoping to evade his attention.

A particularly cruel look came into his eyes. "Now! Let's see what you are made of!" He walked down the line and picked out a girl from the middle. "Step forward," he said. Then he walked down the line and pointed at Pandora "Step forward!". He gestured for them to come forward in front of the lines of students. "Now fight!" he said.

Everyone looked shocked, particularly Pandora and the other girl who had bright red hair.

"I said fight!" said the instructor.

Pandora knew when she was being tested. She had tested enough people herself in her time. She took up a karate stance and faced the red-haired girl. It was time to show what she could do. She decided to enjoy herself.

The other girl clearly had no martial arts training. She stood there awkwardly and looked intimidated by the posture Pandora had taken. She took a step back. Pandora didn't wait. She sensed the uncertainty in the girl so sprang forward, delivering a hard punch to the side of the girl's face. The girl went down. Pandora shuffled back, hands up and watching the red-haired girl to make sure the fight was over. The girl was rolling on the floor, her hands up over her face, clearly in pain and shock.

"What do you think you are doing?!" yelled the instructor at

Pandora.

"I am sorry Sir, I thought you wanted us to fight," said Pandora with alarm. She was thinking: *Oh no! Have I done it again?!*

"I do! So why are you standing there looking like a wet lettuce when you should be on top of her finishing off the job?" he said. "Get on with it!"

Pandora realised suddenly that things were very different here. He actually wanted her to fight. She leapt on the girl and started hitting her whilst she was rolling on the ground. The girl cried and covered her head.

"Enough!" called the instructor. Pandora didn't hear him, she was so intent on the fight. He grabbed her by the back of her shirt and easily pulled her off the girl with the red hair. He flung her to one side "I said enough!". "And you! Stop whining and get back in line" he said to the girl who was crying and bleeding on the floor.

He returned to the line and picked out two more students. They stepped forward. "Fight!" he said.

**Chapter 21**

Another day dawned at the Academy. After breakfast, the students reported to the Summer Dojo as usual. Sensei Goodwin was waiting for them with a big smile.

"Today we have something interesting for you. You will learn to operate in the dark, without sight."

The students looked puzzled. It was a nice bright summer day. Sensei Goodwin laughed. "There is more than one way to experience the dark!". He pulled something that had been tucked in his belt and held it up. It was a long strip of satin. "Blindfolds!"

He tied the long strip of fabric around his head and arranged it so it completely covered his eyes.

He gestured to senior student, John. "Roundhouse and uppercut punches, please! Nice and slow."

John started delivering a series of slow roundhouse punches to either side of Sensei Goodwin's head and uppercut punches to his jaw in a sequence of four strikes – roundhouse right, roundhouse left, uppercut right, uppercut left. The Sensei swung his arms up and down to block each punch.

"Now fast!" he said. John responded by picking up the pace and delivering much faster punches. Sensei Goodwin blocked them all easily.

"And slow again!" said Sensei Goodwin and demonstrated the

slow speed again.

"Stop!" he said to finish.

He removed his blindfold and made a small bow to John, who bowed deep in return and retired to the back of the mat to stand with Bella.

Sensei Goodwin turned to the class. "So you see? You don't need to see in order to defend yourself. But this is a skill that must be developed over time. Don't expect to become expert at it in one day or even during this course. It may take years for you to get really good at it. But we start now and practise often – and then all things are possible!"

"I want you to get into pairs and practise this. Take it in turns to wear the blindfold and keep your punches very slow and gentle. This is not a competition. You are there to help your training partner train. When you bow you are honouring your partner for lending their body to help you train. Always remember that. Take care of each other and train carefully."

The students got into pairs and Bella and John distributed blindfolds to each student.

"These are your blindfolds now," said Sensei Goodwin. "Look after them and always keep them tucked into your belt. They are your first piece of Ninja kit."

Mark raised his hand. Sensei Goodwin nodded to him. Mark spoke up "I can see why we need them for training, but why do

Ninjas need to blindfold people out in the world?"

Sensei Goodwin smiled "Good question! But I suspect you know the answer, Mark. What else could you use a long strip of fabric for?"

"Tying someone up?" asked Mark.

"Absolutely!" said Sensei Goodwin. "Tying your prisoner is a traditional Ninja skill."

Lucy put her hand up. "Carrying herbs?" she asked.

"Yes!" said Sensei Goodwin. "You can use it to carry all sorts of things or tie all sorts of things. It is a very versatile piece of equipment."

Half the students tied their blindfolds and attempted to do the blocking exercise that Sensei Goodwin had demonstrated. There were a lot of giggles. It was funny when they blocked successfully and funny when they missed.

"I can hear a lot of laughter!" said Sensei Goodwin. "That's okay sometimes. It is good to enjoy your training! You are training well and being careful. That's what is important."

"Right!" he said after a while. "It is important that you practise with all sorts of partners in order to develop these skills. So change partners and have another go."

The students changed partners. This time Mark was training with Lucy. He noticed she was very accurate with her blocks and seemed to be almost dreamy and very peaceful. When it was his turn, he tried being dreamy, but it didn't work for him. He just kept missing the blocks. Clearly there was more to it than that. He stopped trying to be dreamy and instead just focussed on trying to hear the movements that indicated that a punch was coming. This was a much more successful strategy for him. He blocked every punch.

"Enough!" called Sensei Goodwin. "Now I am sure I have told you about houses and foundations. I must also tell you this. A lot of good martial artists come to me and tell me they not improving any more. They are good, but can't seem to get any better. They have hit what we call a plateau. Do you know what I say to them? I tell them to go back to their basics and work on their foundations. It is normally a weakness in the foundation that stops progress at any level."

He smiled "So you know what this means, don't you? Standing like a martial artist and moving like a martial artist! Line up and let's do some standing and shuffling!"

## Chapter 22

Sensei Tanaka was waiting for them after lunch with the two senior students Bella and John. "Are we all here?" he asked. "Good! Well, I hope you all brought your new blindfolds with you?"

The students all checked that the satin fabric strips were folded and tucked into their belts. There were various calls of "Yes Sensei!"

"I am going to be very kind to you today," said Sensei Tanaka with a wicked grin that suggested that he might not be at all "I am going to tell you what will happen so you can prepare."

The students looked relieved. They had become accustomed to their Ninja Skills lessons being somewhat surprising.

"I am going to lead you out into the forest. And then you will put on your blindfolds and find your own way home. Does that sound fun?" he asked with a grin.

The students thought it sounded quite impossible but they nodded anyway and said "Yes Sensei".

"Follow me!" he said. "I suggest that you pay particular attention to the path we take and the Landmarks. You may want to build some Waymarks too."

He stopped and stroked the bark of a tree. "Remember! You will be coming back this way without sight. So you must know how the forest feels."

The students started reaching out and touching the trees and bracken as they passed.

"Remember also how the forest smells!" he said "There are different smells everywhere. The bracken smells one way, dried leaves another. The waterways have their own scent too. And the flowers have their own perfume. Experience the forest like a dog – as a symphony of scents."

He kicked through some dried leaves "Remember how the forest sounds. The rustle of the leaves. Listen for the birds and the little animals of the forest. They each have their sounds and each prefers certain areas."

As if on cue, there was a sound of a woodpecker in a large oak tree ahead of them. "Mr Woodpecker loves this tree," said Sensei Tanaka "When you hear Mr Woodpecker in this area, you are probably near this tree." He gestured to the clearing behind the tree. "You have also found your way to a very special place. This is the Green Ninja Dojo where a very special martial artist once trained."

"When your sight is taken by the blindfold, you must rely on all your other senses. With training, these senses will become more and more sensitive. And then you will experience the world in great vibrance!"

After a little further, Sensei Tanaka came to a stop. "Now put your blindfolds on please and try and find your way back to Mr Woodpecker's oak tree."

The students all put on their blindfolds and started off, their hands out in front of them. Some stumbled over sticks and they spread out, all moving off in different directions.

Sensei let them explore for a few minutes before calling "Stop!"

"Take off your blindfolds" he called.

The students all removed their blindfolds. There was laughter when they realised how far wrong most of them had gone.

"I think we will play a different game," said Sensei Tanaka. "Get into pairs. One will wear the blindfold and the other will follow their pair using stealth. The stealth partner must not touch or speak to the blindfold partner unless they are going to hurt themselves. Then as soon as the blindfolded partner is safe again, the stealth partner must become invisible to them again."

The students thought this sounded a lot safer. "This will be even more fun!" said Charlie. Mark put the blindfold on and Charlie readied himself to go into stealth mode. Nearby, Lucy was putting on her blindfold and had paired with Xinia.

They set off, the blindfolded ones treading carefully, reaching out for trees and bracken, sniffing the air and paying close attention to the sounds around them. Meanwhile, the stealth partners crept along close behind them. They didn't need to hide because their partners were blindfolded but they paid close attention to their feet and avoided making a sound.

The blindfolded ones soon felt rather lost and unsure. Then they were rewarded by the sound of the woodpecker. "Mr Woodpecker!" cried Lucy. They all shuffled carefully towards the sound of the woodpecker until their hands were on the large oak tree.

"Well done!" said Sensei Tanaka. "Now swap over with your partners and see if you can find your way home."

## Chapter 23

After the students had gone to bed and the night had drawn on, the Senseis of the Academy all made their way to a secret room in the basement of the building. Each wore bright white robes and carried a Samurai sword. There was something ceremonial about their dress although it was also practical fighting clothing.

They entered a stone chamber that was lit only by candlelight. In the centre of the room was a large white marble table. It was circular and surrounded by twelve tall backed chairs. The headmaster, Professor Ballard sat first, then Sensei Goodwin took one seat, Sensei Tanaka another and the Aikido instructor with the long black hair sat at another. Seven more similarly dressed men and women filled the other seats, some with face coverings. These were the Ninjas who particularly guarded their identity. The last to enter glided in with a flash of white robe and flicker of long white hair. They were assembled. The table seemed to glow as if in resonance with the energy and power of the Senseis around it.

Professor Ballard spoke first "Thank you for assembling today. I thought we might review our candidates and decide what to do with them next."

"We have lost 3 students already, one to irredeemable bad character, another to untameable fear and another because he brought a knife to the school". There were a few raised eyebrows and tutting noises.

"But we have 17 left and some very promising candidates. Let's go through them shall we?" said Professor Ballard.

"First of all, we have a great student, Mark Vardy. He came to use on the recommendation of Sergeant Yeald." There were various nods of recognition and approval from around the table.

"Mark has an excellent character, is passionately committed to becoming a police officer and of course we all knew his father." continued Professor Ballard

"A great man," said Sensei Goodwin.

"Very much missed," said one of the female Senseis.

"A great martial artist," said the Aikido Sensei "If Mark inherits a tenth of his father's skill and character, he will be a great man one day."

"He is doing well in Martial Arts," said Sensei Goodwin.

"And he has the boldness of a lion!" said the Aikido Sensei.

"And he is very inquisitive!" said the Ninja with the long white hair who had entered last.

"One to watch!" said Sensei Tanaka.

Professor looked at his list. "Ah yes, young Charlie!" he said with a smile

"Everyone seems to love Charlie. He gets on well with everyone and talks easily to people," said Sensei Goodwin

"A good team member," said Sensei Tanaka "And he shows a particular interest in stealth."

"He certainly shows many of the personal qualities of a good police officer," said Professor Ballard thoughtfully "How is he doing in martial arts?"

"As good as any" replied Sensei Goodwin "They have done so little, it is very early to tell. But he tries hard and is a pleasure to have in the Dojo."

Professor Ballard returned to his list "Young Lucy" he said with a smile. One of the female ninjas at the table bowed her head and said: "I cannot speak of course."

"Of course Doctor," he said "I hear nothing but excellent reports about Lucy from all the Senseis. She is, of course, far advanced for her years in herbs and medicine. And I hear that she has some interesting extra-sensory talents too. We always knew Lucy was special but she is proving to be even more special then we knew."

Professor Ballard continued "And Xinia is another special candidate. We all know her mother, of course, an exceptional horsewoman and officer."

There were nods and comments of agreement around the table.

"From what I hear, Xinia has inherited her mother's talents with horses and also seems to have extra-sensory talents too. She may prove to be even more extraordinary," said Professor Ballard.

"And fortunately she is nothing like her sister Pandora!" said Sensei Goodwin with a laugh.

"Chalk and cheese indeed!" said Sensei Tanaka.

## Chapter 24

After another uncomfortable night in the dormitory at Shadowlands, Pandora rose to meet another day. Yesterday had been tough. First the fighting, then a lot of running and physical training. They were trying to test their fitness and determination. Pandora smiled to herself. They didn't know who they were dealing with. She knew she had unbreakable determination and good fitness.

She was up and already dressed when the whistle was blown to summon them all to pre-breakfast training. Having woken early, she had time to tie pretty plaits in the side of her hair which met at the back of her head and lay over a river of honey-coloured waves. Instructor Adams was waiting for them, a sadistic gleam in his eyes. Pandora had noticed this was a frequent expression for him. Clearly he enjoyed putting the students through their paces.

"Today we are going to start with a little run to the beach," said the instructor "Follow me!"

He set off at quite a pace and the students ran after him. It wasn't a long run to the beach, but enough to get many of them out of breath at the pace he had set. It was a beautiful beach with golden sand and waves crashing on the shore.

"Now form a line by the water's edge and link arms," he said. The students hurried to obey. Instructor Adams did not like to be kept waiting.

"When I say go, I want you to walk into the sea and stop when I say. Go!" he ordered.

Pandora looked horrified. She had done her hair nicely and dressed nicely. Now she was going to have to walk into the sea? She didn't like the idea of that. But she refused to be the only one to fail to do the task, so she gritted her teeth and got on with it. She linked arms with the girl on one side of her and boy on the other. "Come on!" she growled to them.

The students walked hesitantly into the water. They got in as deep as their chests before the instructor yelled "Stop! Now stay there!"

The students did their best to obey, but it wasn't easy with the waves crashing into them. The water was up to their chests and the waves were splashing over their heads.

None of the students enjoyed this. The water was cold and the experience was frightening. Some of the students were a bit nervous about the water and were worried they would drown or get swept away.

Instructor Adams stood on the beach, daring them to break the chain. It wasn't long before one of the students panicked and broke the chain. He scrambled towards the beach.

"Get back in there!" yelled the instructor. But the boy had had enough and was frightened. He kept crawling up the beach.

"Well get back to your dorm and pack then," said the instructor "You are no good here." His tone was angry and scornful.

The students held fast in the water, wishing their trial was over too.

The waves kept coming, there were a few screams and some students coughing up seawater that they had accidentally swallowed. Instructor Adams watched mercilessly.

After what seemed an age, he snapped "Get out and run back. I don't want to see anyone dawdling on the way home or you won't get breakfast."

Pandora ran back with the others. She was far from impressed to have her nicely done hair wrecked by the sea, but she was pleased with herself. She hadn't broken the chain or given in. She was proving herself every minute she was there.

## Chapter 25

It was the fifth day of training at the Academy and the students had got rather accustomed to reporting to the Summer Dojo for their martial arts lesson. Today they were greeted by the Aikido Sensei.

"Good morning," he said "I don't think I introduced myself last time we met. My name is Marius Silver, although I would hope you would accord me the respect of addressing me as Sensei Silver."

"Good morning Sensei Silver!" the class chorused.

Sensei Silver knelt, sitting back on his heels with his knees apart and gestured to the class to do likewise. The students all knelt and tried to copy his position. He bowed his head down to the mat and the students did so too. Then he turned around and bowed to the picture of O Sensei on the wall. The students shuffled around to face the picture and bowed also. Then they turned to face him again.

"Good! We have some dojo manners now" said Sensei Silver.

He rose and gestured senior student John to take up a place in front of him. "Today we are going to start to learn a little about harmony."

He offered his wrist to John. John came forward and reached to grab it, but as John got close, Sensei Silver stepped sideways and moved his wrist away out of reach. John followed it, still trying to grab it, but it was out of reach and he was off balance. Sensei Silver tapped the back of John's other shoulder and this pushed John beyond the point of balance and into a fall. He rolled over easily, as they had been taught in the previous lesson and was soon back on his feet and coming in to try and grab Sensei's other wrist.

In this way, they repeated the exercise several times. Each time, Sensei turned and brought his wrist just out of reach of John, then tapped the back of his other shoulder and sent him rolling away. It was as if there was an invisible cord between Sensei's wrist and John's hand as he reached for it.

"You try!" said Sensei Silver after a while.

The students got into pairs and tried to emulate what they had seen demonstrated. Mark and Charlie had great fun. It was like a big game for them. Mark offered his wrist and tried to leave it as late as possible before pulling it back from Charlie as he reached for it. Charlie of course tried to beat Mark and grab the wrist.

This game became popular amongst the pairs. There was a lot of laughter.

"Less laughing and more concentration please!" said Sensei Silver.

Lucy and Xinia were having a rather more interesting experience of this exercise. Lucy could see lines of light between her wrist and Xinia's hand. Xinia saw an intense mist of light between hand and wrist and felt a magnetic pull towards Lucy's wrist. As the students around them moved and tumbled, both girls felt the energy of the room rise and saw swirls of light trails.

The girls revelled in the experience at first. It was so pleasant and beautiful! The exercise became like a lovely dance amongst a swirling pool of light. They turned and projected, reached and tumbled.

Then it became a bit too much for them. Both felt overwhelmed by the experience. They stopped and looked at each other, each knowing the other had hit a kind of limit.

Sensei Silver had been watching them closely and was with them in a moment.

"It is different for you, I know," he said. "You have very special gifts but you must learn to control them and not be overwhelmed by what they bring you. Taking control of your breathing will help. And knowing how far you can cope is essential. You were wise to stop. Sometimes you will have to just walk away and be alone. If you can go and sit in nature and breathe deeply, this will be best of all. You must learn to ground your energy. But this is something we can teach you in time."

He called the class to attention. "Let's all take a moment to breathe and think about the role of breath in Aikido," he said, gesturing them back in line.

"Place a hand on your chest and breathe in slowly and deeply," he said. The students copied him as he demonstrated, wondering why he was telling them to do something as obvious as breathing.

"When you breathe out, feel the breath flow out of your body. Completely empty your lungs. Be aware of how much air that was. Now breathe again and this time visualise breathing power into your body and then breathing power out."

"Now follow what I do. Offer your wrist to an imaginary attacker and then breathe in as your turn away and withdraw your hand, filling yourself with power. Then as you tap your attacker's other shoulder, breathe out. Let that breath be the power that projects him."

The class practised this with imaginary attackers. When they appeared to be performing this well, Sensei Silver let them return to practising in pairs.

"This time, try and project your partner without even touching his shoulder. Let your breath be the power that throws them."

The students weren't laughing anymore. They were focussing so hard on throwing their partners with breath. Sensei Silver walked around, correcting the students here and there and watching with general approval. The class was doing much better than he had anticipated. It was very promising.

The breathing and re-focussing had helped Lucy and Xinia. They were concentrating on their breathing as they did the exercise and this was also serving to distract them from the extra-sensory perceptions that complicated it. They were both smiling and clearly enjoying themselves now. Sensei Silver continued to watch them with interest.

## Chapter 26

After lunch, the students reported to the Summer Dojo again and waited for Sensei Tanaka outside. They were expecting a Ninja Skills lesson. At first, there was no sign of him. Then a horse and rider rounded the corner. Sensei Tanaka was sitting on a black horse with a long wavy mane. There was no saddle on the horse and no bridle on his head. In fact, the horse wore no tack at all.

Sensei Tanaka rode the horse round in a circle. The students could not see how he was controlling the horse at all. Then he and the horse stopped and started backing up. Then the horse glided sideways to the left and then sideways to the right. The students gasped. It was a remarkable sight.

Then Sensei Tanaka brought the horse close to them. The horse stopped and he quietly slid off him and then turned and rubbed the horse's neck and back. "Thank you Midnight," he said. Midnight nuzzled him. Sensei Tanaka rubbed Midnight's forehead and smoothed the long forelock of mane that fell from between his ears.

Sensei Tanaka turned to the students "Important Ninja skill! Horsemanship!"

Charlie put his hand up. Sensei Tanaka nodded "Yes Charlie?"

"Are we going to ride horses today Sensei?" he asked.

Sensei Tanaka laughed "All in good time young Charlie! First, you must get to know a horse, become his friend, earn his trust.

Never expect a horse to carry you if he doesn't know and trust you!"

Some of the students looked disappointed. "But we can make a start today!" said Sensei Tanaka "Today we learn to make friends with horses. And if you are selected on this course and join the school next term, then you can learn everything and one day ride." he smiled "Maybe"

The students weren't sure which part of that the "maybe" applied to. Sensei Tanaka spoke in riddles sometimes and it wasn't always easy to understand what he meant. Did he mean that maybe they would be selected? That maybe they would come to the school? That maybe they would learn about horses? Or that maybe they would ride one day?

"Come and meet some new friends," he said to them and set off up the path. Midnight walked alongside him and the students followed behind, but not too close. Many of them knew that it was dangerous to walk close behind a horse.

Sensei Tanaka led them to the stable yard. There were lots of horses in the yard. He assembled the students together and then called Lucy out to stand a little way in front of the crowd. The horses were wandering around freely. They were curious about the new people in the yard. After a while, one came forward and sniffed Lucy. It was a pretty grey mare with gentle eyes and a slightly pink nose. Sensei Tanaka smiled "Ah! Whisper has chosen you" he said. "Let her sniff you and decide how close she wants to be with you."

The horse thoroughly inspected Lucy, who made no move to touch her yet. Lucy was dying to though. She couldn't believe how lucky she was to be chosen by this beautiful creature! Whisper was very interested in Lucy's hands. She nuzzled them. "Is she looking for food?" she asked Sensei Tanaka.

"I think she senses something else," he said. "Horses see many things that we often do not. Let's see how she feels about it if you were to place your hands on either side of her jaws. I think she would like that."

Lucy did as she was bid. Whisper gave a low whickering sound and rested her head into Lucy's hands. They stood there together, girl and horse, for what seemed like a long time. Lucy felt a deep peace warming her. The heat that always seemed to pour from her hands was now flowing into this horse who absorbed it easily. For the first time, Lucy felt something that was hard to describe. It was as if she was finally in balance with the world. She closed her eyes. Before long, her face was next to Whisper's. She felt the warm soft fur against her cheek. This was a magic beyond description! Her breath slowed until she was breathing with the horse, slow and steady.

Presently, Whisper appeared to come out of the trance she seemed to be in. She gave Lucy's arm a nuzzle and then drifted away, back to the herd.

Lucy returned to the students, rather dazed by her experience. She had not expected that at all.

One by one, the students were called forward. Some had similar moments of bonding when a horse chose them. Some students did not attract the attention of any of the horses. When it was Mark's turn, he desperately wanted a horse to come and talk to him. To his disappointment, none seemed to be interested. Sensei Tanaka read the disappointment on his face. "You are trying too hard Mark. The horses sense that you want something from them. Instead, think about what you can give them."

Mark searched his pockets. He had nothing to give them to eat. Sensei Tanaka laughed "They already had their dinner. But there is something else you can give them."

Mark looked puzzled. "Am I right in thinking you have learned a little Tai Chi young man?" asked Sensei Tanaka.

"Yes, Sensei. Mr Liu taught us" replied Mark.

"Well horses love chi!" said Sensei Tanaka. Mark looked confused. What was Sensei saying he should do?

"Show the horses your Tai Chi," said Sensei Tanaka. Mark half-raised an eyebrow. He thought this a strange request. Would the horses want to see his Aikido too?! But he did as he was told.

Mark started going through the Tai Chi form that Mr Liu had taught them. He didn't remember it all very well, but he did his best and just kept moving. Before long he had half a dozen horses standing around him, all fascinated by his movements and fixated on the gap between his hands. He looked at Sensei Tanaka for reassurance. Sensei Tanaka nodded "Continue!"

Mark kept going, his hands floating up and painting the air with his fingers. The horses' heads moved up and down in unison with his hands. Then as he swept his arm slowly around and took up a new position, the horses all swayed with his movement. When he finally came to a stop, the horses edged closer, all wanting to sniff and investigate him. He opened his hands, sensing that this was what they wanted to explore most. The horse's noses sniffed and nuzzled him. He started stroking their faces. They seemed to like it very much. One lowered his head so that Mark's hand rested on his forehead. Mark gently massaged the white starburst on the horse's head. The whole herd seemed to doze off to sleep.

"See!" said Sensei Tanaka, "I said we would make some friends today!"

But Mark barely heard him. He was in a very happy dream with his new horse friends.

# Chapter 27

The early morning dip in the sea had got the day off to a bracing start at Shadowlands. After breakfast, things looked up though for the students. When they reported to Instructor Adams for morning training, he led them to a large building. Inside, to their great excitement, was a line of motorbikes. The bikes were small, scrambler bikes suitable for children of their age and size and designed for off-road riding. Hanging on the handlebars of each was a child-sized motorbike helmet. He told them to take one each and push it outside to the field.

The students couldn't believe their luck! None of them had ever ridden a motorbike before and certainly hadn't expected to get the opportunity at their age.

He took them through the controls of the bike. Then he told them to put the helmets on, get on the bike and start their engines. Pandora's eyes lit up. This was going to be fun!

All the students started their engines. Some felt fairly nervous, others excited. Pandora was definitely one of the excited ones.

"Now put it into gear and take it for a ride," said Instructor Adams. He didn't bother warning them not to go too fast or look out for stones and uneven ground. He reasoned that they would work it out one way or another and was a great believer in learning by mistakes. At least, he thought others should learn by mistakes. He didn't always apply his harsher judgements to himself.

One of the girls, a small girl called Jenny, set off a few yards on the bike, stopped, tried again and then stopped and froze. She was scared.

"Open up that throttle and get on with it!" roared Instructor Adams at her. He had no time for fear.

Jenny tried again. The bike shot forward, she lost control and toppled over to one side. Fortunately, her leg went out to save her and she wasn't actually moving very fast. She had just thought she was.

"Are you going to ride that bike or just sit on it all day?" yelled the instructor rather meanly.

"I'm scared. I am going to fall off!" she sobbed back. The more he yelled, the more stressed she felt and the less she could do it. She just wanted to get off this horrible machine.

Instructor Adams marched up to her, grabbed the handlebar and hissed in her ear. "Ride the bike or leave the school, it's up to you."

Jenny closed her eyes, as if that would help. Then she took a deep breath and tried once more. This time she was luckier. The bike pulled away more smoothly this time. She just about managed to hold her nerve and keep the bike moving across the field, after the others and away from the hissing instructor.

Meanwhile, Pandora was streaming across the field, her honey blonde hair floating on the wind where it emerged under her helmet. She was racing with the most competitive of the boys. It hadn't taken her long to master the controls of the bike and she had good balance from her years of horse riding. She was as fearless on a motorbike as she was on a horse.

Instructor Adams noted Pandora's confidence and competitiveness. He smiled. She was going to be a good student and maybe a useful asset one day. He stood watching and let the students just play and race on the bikes all morning. The point of the day was to get them riding the bikes and confident in doing so. They could do that without his intervention. He watched Jenny. He knew she was pretending to be more confident than she felt. But at least she hadn't crumbled in the end. He had thought she would.

Eventually, he blew a whistle and summoned the students back to him. Once they had returned, he briefed them on the afternoon's activities.

"You have all had a chance to get to know your bike. So this afternoon we are going to put your bike riding to the test. There is going to be a race and whoever comes in first will be excused from the final exercise of the day."

Pandora put her hand up. Instructor Adams raised an eyebrow "Yes Pandora?" he said with dangerously exaggerated politeness that they all knew he did not mean.

"What's the final exercise of the day?"

"I thought you might all like another dip in the sea," he said with a sadistic smile. There was a ripple of barely suppressed horror from the students.

"If you don't want another swim, you had better win!" he said "But there will only be one winner. Coming second won't do anyone any good. Now put your bikes back in the building, get to lunch and be back here in an hour"

The students went to lunch, grumbling amongst themselves at the thought of being put in the cold sea again. "I only just got dry from this morning!" complained one boy. "I don't stand a chance of winning," said Jenny miserably.

The students were so busy grumbling that they hadn't noticed that Pandora was not with them. Pandora meanwhile had returned to the bike building, slipped in and was looking around the area at the end of the building where all the maintenance equipment was. She was careful to be very quiet as she rummaged around, looking for a plastic pipe and a container. "Yes!" she hissed under her breath when she found what she was looking for – a thin, clear siphon tube and a couple of fuel cans.

Pandora went to the nearest bike and very carefully siphoned off all but a small amount of fuel at the bottom of its fuel tank. Then she went to the next bike and did the same. She worked along the line until she had nearly drained the tanks of every bike except her own. Then she hid the siphon tube and fuel containers back where she had found them. Then she hurried off to lunch and slipped quietly into the food hall. No-one had noticed she hadn't been there with the rest of the students.

After lunch, the students all got their bikes out again for the big race. Instructor Adams pointed out the route of the race to them. They were to follow a track that wound around a couple of fields and then race back down the middle of the field they started from.

When the instructor blew his whistle to start the race, they all flew away from the start line. They raced hard up the field, nearly running into each other. Jenny held back. She already knew she couldn't win this, so decided not to have a bike accident as well as a soak in the sea this afternoon. The most competitive of the riders cut the corners very tight. Most got away with it, but a few slipped their bike on the corners and fell off. The remaining riders sped off up through the next field. A couple more corners followed and there were a few collisions that eliminated more riders. Then something strange seemed to happen. One by one, their bikes spluttered to a stop. By the time the leaders made it to the start field and the finishing line was in sight, only six or so remained. And they too gradually fell away, one at a time.

Jenny had been taking things slow and hadn't been so heavy on the fuel use as the others. So the small amount of fuel in her tank went further than that of the others. And she had held back at the corners so as to avoid collisions or slipping her bike.

They were halfway home across the field. Pandora couldn't resist looking back to see if her plan had worked. She was delighted to see it was just her and Jenny left and that all the other riders had stopped. She knew she was going to win! Jenny was quite a way

131

behind her still.

A hundred metres from the finish, Pandora looked over her shoulder again and then punched the air in victory. This turned out to be a mistake. At that moment, the front wheel of her bike hit a stone. With one hand in the air, she stood no chance of keeping control. The bike slid from under her and she was sent flying.

Jenny was still going slow, but she passed Pandora as she sprawled on the field. She kept going, not knowing how many there were behind her. Pandora could see that Jenny was almost crawling along on her bike. She scrambled to her feet, picked up her bike and fired it up again. Then she took off after Jenny. There was still time and Jenny was so slow!

But it was too late. Jenny puttered slowly across the finish line and Pandora came streaking in behind her, fast but too late.

Instructor Adams laughed. It was very obvious to him that Pandora had emptied the other student's fuel tanks. If she had been really smart, she might have realised how guilty she looked having the only bike with a full tank. But he appreciated her competitive spirit and willingness to do whatever it takes to succeed.

Jenny was stunned. How on earth could she have won that race?! She was such a nervous rider and had ridden so slowly.

The other students gradually returned to the start line, pushing their bikes and some limping on bruised and scuffed knees.

"Put your bikes away!" ordered Instructor Adams "And let's go for a little swim shall we?!"

The students did as they were told and then ran miserably down to the sea. Pandora was utterly fuming. She had had such a great plan and it had gone so badly wrong. Jenny sat on the beach and was made to watch as the others were made to stand in the sea again and get buffeted by the waves. When they finally were allowed to emerge, Pandora stamped past Jenny and hissed "That was mine! You will regret this!"

Instructor Adams heard her threat. He smiled to himself and said nothing. There was no reason not to allow a bit of competition and rivalry to emerge - and that snivelling Jenny girl needed the kind of toughening up that Pandora would probably give her.

## Chapter 28

After the adventures of the day, the Shadowlands students were all keen to get to their dinner. But they had to go and dry off and change first, after ending their afternoon in the sea. Pandora was slower than the rest. She was still fuming from having lost the race and ending up in the sea, despite all she had done. Pandora was also quite vain and liked to make her hair look pretty before going to dinner. So by the time the other students were finishing their meal, she was only just starting her pudding, which was a strawberry custard.

As the students passed her on the way out of the hut, some of them started muttering "Thank you Pandora!" in a rather unfriendly way. The mutterings got louder and louder as each was emboldened by the students who had gone before them. By the time it came to a rather aggressive girl called Melissa at the end of the line, the mutterings had become loud and angry snarls. The students were all very angry with her for draining the fuel from their tanks, causing them a few accidents and causing them to lose the race. They blamed her also for the second dip in the sea they had been subjected to, even though that wasn't really her fault. Instructor Adams had said that would be happening anyway. It wasn't as if she had escaped it either!

Melissa growled "Thank you Pandora!" and shoved Pandora's face into her bowl of custard. There was an explosion of pink custard and custard soaked gold hair as Pandora emerged quickly from her pudding bowl. Everyone laughed. She looked quite ridiculous with her face all covered in pink custard and globules of it falling off her.

If there was one thing that Pandora really couldn't stand, it was being laughed at. She leapt to her feet and flew after Melissa, lashing out at her in blind anger. Her punches hit thin air because she couldn't see through the custard. She looked even more ridiculous now and the students just laughed louder and harder at her. Pandora screamed with fury.

At that moment, Instructor Adams appeared and grabbed Pandora's wrist. "Come!" he barked, dragging her away firmly. He grabbed Melissa's wrist with his other hand and marched them both off to his office.

"Stand!" he barked again. The two girls stood side by side, itching to fight with each other again.

"Now listen carefully," he said "I don't know what that was about, although I could make a pretty good guess. I don't actually care what that was about. But I can tell you what it was. It was ineffective."

He started pacing slowly backwards and forwards as he lectured them. "I can tolerate many things, but one thing I absolutely cannot stand is students being ineffective. That's not what we train you to be."

He looked at them piercingly. He knew they didn't understand and still just wanted to fight with each other.

"I know you are angry and you want to fight. Anger is good if it is turned to something useful. Fighting is not only good, it is necessary and important. But we only use our anger and fighting in strategic ways. We don't just lash out because we feel annoyed. That is not how a ninja operates. We are very controlled. We take our revenge when it is strategic to do so. Our enemies do not know we are there and they don't know what we have done. We slip in. We are effective. Then we slip out. Silent as the night."

He continued "The point is that we are effective, not lashing around covered in custard. Nor do we push people in custard – unless we can do it silently and get away with it! Do you understand?"

The girls nodded. Pandora was feeling sulky still and Melissa was still blaming Pandora for everything she hadn't liked about her day.

"Let me explain this another way," said Instructor Adams "I don't need you to be friends. We don't encourage you to have friends here. I don't even want you to be nice to each other. We really despise people being nice!" Here he practically spat the word "nice" out in disgust at the notion.

"What I want you to do and what this school needs you to do is to learn to be effective at working together. We need to be able to send you out into the world to do a job and know you will co-operate effectively, work effectively, be effective!"

"If you can master the art of working effectively with people you cannot stand; and if you can do this without them having the slightest idea of how you really feel, you will find you can be very effective in many situations," he said.

He stopped his pacing and looked at them with a cool and steady gaze. "To become a great ninja, you must master your emotions. You must eliminate all but the coldest of anger, rage and hatred. And you must be so cold in these emotions that no-one can know that you feel them. The angrier you feel inside, the more cool and controlled you must appear on the outside. A ninja hides his feelings as cleverly as he hides himself."

"Now go to bed. And don't let me catch you wasting time and effort on ineffective squabbling. Understood?!" he snapped.

"Yes Sir," they both said, trying already to be level in their emotions and neutral in their response.

## Chapter 29

Another day dawned at the Academy. Today the students had been told to dress in their Ninja Skills camouflaged judogis. They met Sensei Tanaka outside the Summer Dojo as usual.

"Today we have a new challenge for you!" he said with excitement. "Today you will learn to navigate!"

Bella and John handed out a map and compass to each student. Sensei Tanaka held up the map. He pointed to a spot at the bottom of the map. "The Academy is here!" he said. The students all unfolded their maps and looked for the spot where the Academy was on their own maps. There were cries of "Where is it?" and "Found it!". When everyone seemed happy that they had found the Academy on the map, Sensei Tanaka pointed to a location at the top of his map. It had a little symbol on it.

"This is where you will navigate to. It is a tall brick tower. You must find your way here by five o'clock. We will be waiting for you and you will be driven back to the school. But if you are late, you will have to walk all the way home again and you will have failed the test!"

"Understand?!" he asked. The students all chorused "Yes Sensei"

Sensei Tanaka gave them a big grin and said: "Make the Academy proud today!". With that, he strode off into the forest and disappeared.

"Are we meant to do this on our own?" asked Charlie.

"He didn't say so," said Mark, who always paid attention to any rules that were set. "He just said we have to get to the tower by five o'clock."

They all poured over the map. "It doesn't look very far to the tower," said Xinia. Lucy checked the scale on the map. "It's only about five miles. I don't think that will take us all day to walk."

Some of the others had already set off into the forest. Mark, Charlie, Lucy and Xinia hurried off after them. At various points, some of the students checked their compass and maps. They all agreed that they needed to take the main path North through the forest. They could see a road ran across from west to east about a couple of miles ahead of them. It was a good landmark, so they headed towards it.

After a while, they came to the road. It wasn't a busy road, just a narrow country road that only saw the occasional car. To their surprise, there were horses all over the road. They didn't look like forest ponies. They were more finely bred than that.

"I don't think these horses are meant to be out here," said Xinia. She was right. A farmer came down the road towards the students.

"Hello," he said "Do you have a few minutes to help me herd my horses back into their field, please? It would be so much easier with a team of you."

139

A few of the students pretended not to hear him. They recognised that this was a chance to get ahead of the others. They kept on walking. But most of the students stayed and agreed to help the farmer.

"Of course we will Sir," said Mark. Then he turned to his fellow students and said: "Let's fan out and then we can just close the fan down and herd them back."

"Let's take it slowly and gently though," said Xinia. "We want the horses to stay calm and walk back to their field quietly"

"I can see you young people know what you are doing," said the farmer "I really am most grateful for your help. This little road leads out to the main road a mile or so that way. If the horses went that way, they could get hurt."

The students spread out. Some stayed behind the horses and some arced around ahead of the horses until they were completely surrounded. Then they very quietly and slowly herded the horses back to their field.

"Thank you!" called the farmer, waving over his shoulder as he went into the field with his horses and closed the gate.

Charlie looked at his watch "We had better get moving. We lost a bit of time there and some of the others went ahead."

They checked the map again. The road they were on would lead them west towards another good track that they could take up towards the tower. They could maybe regain a bit of time simply through having a clear route to take. So they walked along the road. They rounded a corner and came up behind an old lady who was struggling along with a shopping trolley and bags. She was clearly having a difficult time.

"Oh no!" thought Charlie. Here was someone else they would have to help. They were going to start running a bit late. He and the others looked at each other. They all knew what it could cost them, but they couldn't leave an old lady struggling.

"May we help you Madam?" asked Mark "You seem to have rather a lot of shopping to carry"

"Oh how kind young man!" she said and gratefully allowed the students to take her bags and trolley.

"I just live along here a bit. It isn't far," she said.

It may not have been far, but the old lady was bent over and she moved extremely slowly. The students were tempted to run ahead and just drop the bags at her house, but that would have seemed very rude. The last thing Sensei Tanaka had said was "Make us proud!". Lucy had noticed that. She knew Sensei Tanaka said all things for good reason. The Academy would want them to be polite and help this lady properly.

So the students walked extremely slowly with the old lady, carrying her bags and wheeling her shopping trolley. Eventually, they arrived at her cottage, which was a very sweet stone cottage with roses over the door and a garden crammed full of every type and shade of plant.

"Thank you so much!" said the old lady. "Would you like to come in for some lemonade?"

"We would love to but we have to be at the stone tower by five o'clock," said Mark.

"That's only a couple of miles away," said the old lady "You have more than enough time. Come and sit in my garden and have some lemonade and biscuits. I baked some this morning. I must have known you were coming!"

"Now go round the side to the back garden and I will bring some out to you," she said, suddenly seeming a lot more able to pick up and carry her bags into the house.

The students went around the side of the house, brushing past lush beds of flowers, the scent of roses and lavender heavy on the air. Lucy appreciated the garden particularly. She spotted some medicinal herbs that her mother used sometimes. She pointed out some of them to the others. "Oh look – Calendula," she said, "My mother uses that in a lot of medicine."

"What does your Mother use it for?" asked Mark, who was beginning to take a bit of an interest in herbs and medicine.

"It's good for skin problems" replied Lucy "She uses it for other things too."

The path led round to a lovely grass lawn and a table and chairs. There were not enough chairs for all of them, so most of them sat on the grass. The lady appeared. She was as good as her word.

She brought a tray of glasses, a big jug of rose coloured lemonade and a big tin of home-baked chocolate chip biscuits.

It was a warm day and the students very much enjoyed the refreshing drink. The biscuits were delicious.

"Where do you all come from?" asked the lady

"We are from the Academy," said Lucy "We are out on a navigation exercise today."

"It's lucky we were out today," said Charlie "It meant we were here to help you. If we had come out tomorrow, we wouldn't have been here."

The old lady smiled "It's good to be in the right place at the right time, isn't it? There are no accidents in life. We are all exactly where and when we ought to be."

Mark thought he detected an unusual kind of wisdom in her words. It reminded him of something Mr Liu had said about time. He couldn't quite remember it. It was something about only being able to control what you understand. Nevertheless, the subject of time reminded him that they were on an exercise and had to be to the tower by five o'clock. He rose.

"Thank you very much for the lemonade and biscuits, Madam. But we really must be going now," he said.

"I am Mrs Green by the way. Would you mind if I took a photograph of you all before you left?" she asked. "I would like to remember the lovely young people who helped me today."

They all agreed. She went back to the house and returned with an old-looking camera. She took a quick photograph of them all sitting in the lawn drinking lemonade. "What a lovely memory!" she said "Thank you"

The students reluctantly tore themselves away from the lovely lemonade and tasty biscuits. "Thank you Mrs Green!" they all chorused to her as they left.

"You are welcome. Do call again!" she said with a warm smile.

As they filed off up the road, the old lady picked up the telephone in her house. She dialled a number without looking it up "They have just left. Not all of them helped. I took a photo of those who did. Farmer John was very happy for their help too!" she chuckled.

The students checked their watches and maps. It was now two o'clock. They had three hours left to get to the tower. The old lady had been right. It should only be a couple of miles away. They turned off the road and back into the wild forest, following the path they had identified earlier.

They were about halfway to their target location when they saw a loose dog just wandering around on the path they were walking. There didn't seem to be any sign of an owner nearby.

Mark knelt down and looked at the dog. He really loved dogs. This one was a small German Shepherd Dog and was a female. She had soft, friendly ears and seemed both pleased to meet him but anxious to be away from her humans. Mark reached out and tickled her chest. She clearly liked this and pushed closer to him, allowing him to stroke up her shoulders and towards her head.

Mark gently reached for the collar around her neck. The collar had a tag on it. It had a name on it and a phone number. The name was "Sasha".

"Hello Sasha," he said. The dog wagged her tail. "Where are your Mum and Dad?"

Sasha looked a bit sad. She was a clever dog and knew a lot of human language. She certainly knew the words "Mum" and "Dad".

The other students started looking around for the dog's owners, calling out for them. But there was no sign of anyone and no reply from their calls.

"We can't leave her here," said Mark "We have to take her to a police station"

One of the other boys looked at his watch "We don't have time. The police station is a couple of miles away in the village. We don't have time to take the dog there and get back to the tower."

"Well I'm going to help her," said Mark "That's more important. If we leave her out here, she might starve or get hit by a car or injured in some other way. And I bet her folks at home are worried sick and searching for her."

"I'll come with you," said Charlie. "And me," said Xinia and Lucy. "We all will".

145

"We can't all go or Sensei Tanaka won't know what happened. You four go and we will go ahead and tell him. I hope you make it." said the other boy and he and the others headed off on the trail towards the tower.

Mark looked at the dog. "We need a lead or we will lose her," he said.

Lucy grinned and produced the ninja blindfold scarf she had tucked in her belt. "Sensei Tanaka said these have many uses. I bet he didn't expect us to use it as a dog lead!"

"That will be perfect," said Mark. He tied the scarf to the dog's collar. "Come on girl! Let's take you home!"

Sasha heard her favourite word, or rather one of her favourite words "Home". She set off, leading the little crowd of four back towards the road and then along it to the village.

The walk took a while, but it didn't take them long to find the police station once they were there. The village had a main street of about half a mile long, dotted with little shops here and there, all built in golden stone. The police station was opposite the church, the other side of what looked like a war memorial in the middle of the road. Mark imagined that this village looked like a scene from a Christmas card when it snowed.

They went into the police station and led Sasha up to the Sergeants desk. "We found this dog, Sir," said Mark "She was lost in the forest. Her name is Sasha and there is a phone number on the collar."

146

"Her owners are going to be absolutely delighted," said the Sergeant "They were in earlier to report her being missing. They were extremely upset and worried. Sit down a moment and I will telephone them."

He picked up the telephone receiver on his desk and dialled a number from his deskbook. "We have your dog, Sasha, here at the station. Some children found her and brought her in."

Mark could hear cries of delight and relief from the phone.

"Can I take your names please?" said the Sergeant. "We have to have it for the records."

Mark stood to attention and delivered the names to the Sergeant as if giving one of his daily reports to Sergeant Yeald back home. He thought of him a moment. He missed him and he missed giving his reports to him. He wondered how things were at home.

"Now we really must be going Sir," said Mark. "We have to be at the stone tower by five o'clock or we will fail our navigation exercise for the Academy and it is quarter to five now"

The Sergeant looked at him doubtfully. "You wouldn't make it even if you ran"

He smiled "But you have been such heroes and I know Sasha's people wouldn't want you to fail your test."

"Go outside and wait a moment," he said.

The students went outside. They looked at their watches. There were only twelve minutes left now. There was no way they could make it.

Then there was a jangling of a bell and a police car came round the corner. A police constable lent over and threw the passenger door open. "Jump in!" he said, "We will get you there on time!"

The students wasted no time in scrambling into the car. Then they set off, with blue lights flashing and the sirens blaring.

They arrived at the tower with just two minutes to spare. "Thank you Sir!" they all called as they fell out of the car and ran to the tower.

Sensei Tanaka had a big smile on his face "It looks like some of you had an interesting adventure today!"

## Chapter 30

Long after the students went to bed, the Senseis met to review their progress. The round table glowed again in resonance with the chi of the assembled martial artists. Each was a master in his or her own art. Each was powerful beyond measure. Together they were a force that challenged the laws of physics.

Sensei Silver spoke first. "After we last met, I took them for Aikido and taught them a little harmony. I introduced them to the idea of breath throws. They are such beginners of course. I didn't expect a lot. I am pleased to say they surprised me. After the usual initial giggles, they settled down and worked hard. Some did particularly well."

Professor Ballard spoke "Xinia and Lucy?"

Sensei Silver nodded. "Yes, their abilities are really beginning to blossom and find application. If they train as they should, I think we can do remarkable things with them."

Sensei Goodwin nodded too "I agree. With their gifts, it is a very good thing that they ended up here. It would have been such a waste for them if they had stayed out in the world. Those gifts would have fizzled out, got them into trouble or made them crazy."

"We must look after them" agreed Professor Ballard "How about the others? How did they do with the Aikido?"

Sensei Silver tilted his head and gave a half nod "They did well.

Mark and Charlie will do well because they train hard and have a good degree of natural ability. The two Scottish brothers, James and Malcolm, seem particularly talented with the physical aspects of martial arts."

Sensei Goodwin chimed in "Yes, I noticed that too." He chuckled "I think they must come from good Scottish warrior stock!"

"That bodes well," said one of the other Senseis thoughtfully.

Professor Ballard consulted his paperwork. "Sensei Tanaka, how did they get on with the horses?".

Sensei Tanaka grinned "They all loved them of course. Who wouldn't?! Several of them had special moments. Lucy did of course. The surprise though was that Mark did too. He is one of the most down to earth of our students. I would not have expected him to connect in more than an obvious way. But the horses were mesmerised by his Tai Chi."

"Tai Chi?" asked Professor Ballard, surprised "I wonder where he learned that?"

"I don't think we have to look very far for that," said Sensei Tanaka with an amused look. The other Senseis chuckled too.

"So, the Navigation Challenge. That was interesting!" said Professor Ballard. He rummaged in his file and produced a large photo. He laid it on the table. It was a photo of a group of their students sitting around on a lawn drinking lemonade and eating biscuits.

Sensei Goodwin laughed "Mrs Green struck again I see!"

"Yes. And she said that Farmer John was glad of the assistance of a good number of students too." said Professor Ballard.

The Senseis looked at the faces in the photo. These were the ones who had passed the first two tests of the day. They were unsurprised to see most of the faces there.

Sensei Tanaka spoke again "Only four passed the final test though."

"That was disappointing," said Professor Ballard "Although we might make allowances for the ones who decided to go ahead and let you know what happened."

"We might," agreed Sensei Tanaka

"Some students are already distinguishing themselves from the pack," said Sensei Goodwin.

"We will have to see how they do in the final assessment challenge," said Professor Ballard "talking of which, I think we can expect our friends at Shadowlands to make an appearance as they have on other years."

There were a few eye rolls and head shakes from around the table. The Senseis were not amused by the disruptions that Shadowlands tried to make at this point each year.

"Will we stop them this year?" said Sensei Silver in a voice that suggested he might enjoy doing that.

"We cannot let them think they can interrupt our exercise," said Sensei Goodwin

"And it is good to let our candidates face some real opposition in order to test them fully," said another Sensei

"We can't let it get out of hand or go too far though," said Professor Ballard.

"Well we can watch and step in if it becomes necessary," said Sensei Tanaka, who had been planning to watch from the shadows anyway. He liked to observe the students closely on these exercises in order to see how they did when they thought they weren't being observed.

"Yes," said Professor Ballard, "I think this will require most of us to be present, one way or another."

He turned to Sensei Tanaka "Have you decided on the challenge yet?"

"Pretty much," said Sensei Tanaka "It will be a photograph treasure hunt! They will be put in teams of four, given a camera and a list of things that they must find and photograph"

"I am guessing these things will be in various locations around the forest?" asked Sensei Goodwin.

"Oh yes!" said Sensei Tanaka "And some will be hard to find. They will need to rely on the friends they have made and the things they have noticed. They will have to be patient to find some things. They will have to climb to find others. And they will have to work together. We will see how they do that and find out what they have learned."

**Chapter 31**

Sensei Goodwin was waiting for the students the next morning in the Summer Dojo. "Good morning everyone," he said with a broad smile.

"Good morning Sensei Goodwin," they all replied.

"Today we will learn about breakaways," said Sensei Goodwin. The students looked at each other. They liked the sound of that.

Sensei Goodwin beckoned one of the Scottish brothers on to the matt. It was James, the older of the two. The other students were a little envious that he was the first one of them to be called out to assist a Sensei in a demonstration. But they didn't know what was coming and were also a bit relieved not to be facing the uncertainty. James was a tall and powerfully built boy, but he was still small compared to Sensei Goodwin and they all felt quite sure that Sensei Goodwin could do terrible things to a giant if he wanted to.

But Sensei Goodwin merely extended his right arm as if offering a handshake. "Grab my wrist," he said to James.

James did as he was told and gripped Sensei Goodwin's wrist. Sensei Goodwin's arm then seemed to float effortlessly upwards out of James's grip. The students all looked amazed, but none more so than James himself.

"Let's do that again shall we?" said Sensei Goodwin and offered his wrist again to James who grabbed it hard. Again, Sensei's wrist floated up out of the grip.

"Do you want to have a go?" said Sensei Goodwin, slightly wickedly. He knew they would try the wrong thing and that it wouldn't work. But it was educational for them to explore what wouldn't work before learning what would.

The students got into pairs and took it in turns to grab each other's wrists. A series of tug-o-wars ensued across the dojo as they all tried to pull their wrists out of the grip of their partner.

Sensei Goodwin clapped his hands and the students all retreated to a line across the edge of the dojo.

"Now you have explored what won't work, I will be kind and tell you what will," he said with a smile.

"Where you are all going wrong is that you are fighting your attacker. If he is stronger, you will always lose if you do this. So don't fight. Don't pull back against his grip. Instead, keep your elbow at your side and let your wrist float up. Your thumb will lead your hand out through the opening in his hand. You don't have to use force to do this. Just take it upwards. But definitely don't pull back against the grip or you will fail."

"Now give it another try!" he said.

The students got back in their pairs and this time did the technique as he had shown them. There were cries of triumph from around the dojo as they discovered they could float their wrist out of the grip.

Sensei Goodwin clapped again and they returned to the dojo edge to listen to him.

"I am going to tell you an important secret now," he said, dropping his voice to a whisper. The students all lent forward slightly, very keen to hear this secret.

"The secret is this" whispered Sensei Goodwin "Nothing is what it seems. You need never believe the situation that is put to you. In this case, the situation that is put is that a strong person has your wrist. You don't have to believe that. You can see his hand on your wrist of course. But he doesn't have it. There is almost always an opening in the field of energy and possibility. And when you can't see one, you can create one."

The students looked mystified. They didn't really understand.

"I can tell you all this, but you won't understand it until you discover it and experience it yourselves," he said.

"Imagine the front of a house," said Sensei Goodwin "Where is the opening in the energy field of that?"

Mark's hand shot up. Sensei Goodwin nodded to him. "The front door Sensei!" said Mark.

"That's right," said Sensei Goodwin. "And if there was no door?"

"The windows?" asked Mark

"Indeed," said Sensei Goodwin "And if there were no windows?"

Charlie's hand shot up. Sensei Goodwin turned to him. "You could get a big truck and drive it through the wall and make a hole in it!" said Charlie, imagining doing just that with great excitement at the idea. In his head, the truck was very large and yellow and it was him that was driving it through the wall.

"Yes!" exclaimed Sensei Goodwin "If there is no hole, you make a hole!"

Xinia raised her hand. "Yes Xinia?" asked Sensei Goodwin who knew what her question would be before she asked it.

"How do you make a hole in a person's energy field?" she asked.

"Well, I am glad you asked that," he said. "If their hand is so big that it completely encircles your wrist and there is no way you can find a gap between his thumb and fingers, then you might need to make a hole in that field because none exists. So what you can do then is make a hole in the energy field somewhere else. Does anyone have any ideas about how we might do that?"

Jame's brother Malcolm put his hand up. He was inclined to very literal ways of looking at things and all this talk of energy fields was hard for him to understand. "Would you poke them Sensei?" he asked. The other students laughed. The thought of poking their fingers into an attacker was funny.

"You may well all laugh, but that would be one way to do it!" said Sensei Goodwin. "If you were to poke someone where it hurts, or hit or kick them, then their mind will go to the part of their body that you hurt and they will lose interest in holding on

157

to you so hard."

"So if someone grabs you so hard and has a hand so big you can't float your wrist out of it, then give their shin a kick. Then they will open their grip on your hand and a hole will emerge in their energy field for your wrist to float up out of."

"I am not going to ask you to practise that for real," he said "I don't want you hurting each other and you will do if you kick each other. All you can do is practise the idea of kicking someone without actually doing it. But we can return to that when I have a bit more confidence that you won't hurt each other."

"Let's try another breakaway," he said. "This one is called the Pray and Push"

He offered his wrist to James again and told him to grab it with both hands. This time, instead of floating his wrist up out of the grip, he reached his other hand under James's hands and put his palms together as if praying. Then he turned his body to the left and swept his praying hands up in a circle before turning back to the right and then pushing James's arms away.

"See?" he said "Pray" he put his hands together "And Push!" he swept his hands around in the half circle and pushed his hands away.

"Before you start this one, I will tell you the secret to it. You must use the power of your entire body. So don't just stand there with your feet glued to the floor and your body stiff" he acted out

158

what he was describing with exaggerated posture.

"No! You must move your body first to the left and then turn it and sweep back to the right. I want to see your hand moving through the biggest circle you can make. You will have to use your whole body to do that and that is what will make it powerful and effective."

He looked along the line of students "Some of you will be big and powerful one day. Some of you will always be small. But you can be powerful too!" he said, "You must all learn to engage the power of your whole body in the movements you make."

"Now give that a try!" he said with a grin and watched with pleasure as the students did their best to emulate what he had shown them and implement what he had told them.

## Chapter 32

In the afternoon, they met with Sensei Tanaka outside the Summer Dojo for their Ninja Skills lesson. He was waiting for them with a small rucksack at his side and a groundsheet laid out in front of him.

"Tomorrow you will embark on your final assessment exercise," he said. "The exercise will involve a treasure hunt in the forest!"

The students all looked excited. Charlie raised his hand "What sort of treasure Sensei?"

"Ah hah! That's the interesting thing!" said Sensei Tanaka "You will be hunting photographs!"

Charlie looked confused and asked, "Won't they get wet if it rains?"

Sensei Tanaka laughed. "No! You won't be finding photographs, you will be taking them. I will give you a list of things you must photograph in the forest and then you must go out and find them and take a photograph of them."

"That sounds very easy," said Mark suspiciously. "Is that really all we have to do Sensei?"

"Ah, well it is only as easy as finding these things. You don't know what they are yet. They might be hard to find" he smiled mysteriously.

Sensei Tanaka continued "There may be a few other

complications that you will encounter. You must take all these photos and return home without getting captured by any of the senior students who will pretend to be the enemy. So you must move with stealth through the forest. You must be silent and invisible, using all the techniques you have been taught!"

Charlie's face lit up. He loved doing stealth. He grinned at Mark with excitement, who grinned back. They were going to have a brilliant time doing this!

"Now get into teams," said Sensei Tanaka "There should be two teams of four and two teams of five."

Lucy, Xinia and Nell looked at each other. They wanted to be together. Nell linked arms with Gina too. Nell had become very friendly with Gina recently. Gina was an excellent gymnast who loved the physical side of their training. They decided that they would be a team of four.

Mark and Charlie looked to the Scottish brothers, James and Malcolm. They all nodded at each other and grinned at the girls. It was going to be a boys versus girls race to get those photographs and complete the treasure hunt!

The rest of the students organised themselves into groups of both boys and girls. There had been quite a few friendships formed over the last week and they all looked forward to doing the treasure hunt with their new friends.

"Excellent!" exclaimed Sensei Tanaka "Next we must assemble

and check kit!"

He started unpacking his rucksack and laying out all the contents on the groundsheet in a very neat and organised way. He pointed out the various items as he did, including ropes and a climbing harness, a first aid kit, a food box, a bottle of water and a spare pair of socks.

"Why do you have a spare pair of socks in there?" asked Nell.

Sensei Tanaka laughed "Someone always ends up stepping in a river!"

The students laughed with him. They decided they would take an extra pair of socks too.

"This is what I would pack," he said. "But you may pack whatever you like. You will be given one camera per team and that is what you must use to capture all the photographs in the challenge. So someone has to carry that in their pack too."

"As well as hunting for photographs and evading capture by the senior students, you will also be camping out overnight. Has anyone done that before?" he asked. A few hands went up.

Sensei Tanaka smiled "Next time I ask, you will all have done it!". The students looked even more excited.

"We will be kind to you though. You don't have to carry your camping equipment. We will meet you near the old tower tomorrow night with all the camping equipment and food to make tomorrow night's dinner" he explained.

Mark looked relieved. He was very keen on the subject of dinner and had been wondering where his food would fit into the day's events.

"You have a big day tomorrow," said Sensei Tanaka "A big couple of days in fact. So you may have the rest of the afternoon to yourselves after you have packed your rucksacks for tomorrow. I suggest that you get an early night and wake up ready to take on this challenge. This is your last chance to show us who you are and what you can do. Do not under-estimate it!"

With this, he turned to go and said: "If you would like to follow me, I will take you to the equipment stores and you can pick out what you would like to put in your rucksacks for tomorrow."

He led them up the path to a building behind the main house. "This is the equipment store. You may choose what you wish to take. But remember! You have to carry it all day for at least two days. So take only what you think you will need. I do suggest that you start with collecting a rucksack though!" he chuckled "You will find it hard to carry everything otherwise!"

The students each selected a rucksack from a wall that had a big array of pegs, each of which held a rucksack. Then they turned to the aisles of shelving which contained an array of equipment.

They tried to remember what Sensei Tanaka had laid out on his groundsheet. Mark grabbed a climbing rope and harness. He couldn't imagine why he might need these, but clearly Sensei Tanaka had thought it a necessary item of kit. Charlie did likewise, thinking that Mark was probably wise in this.

163

Lucy asked Sensei Tanaka "Can I take my healing herbs with me?"

Sensei Tanaka nodded "Yes. If you want to. That would be a very good idea. Anything can happen in a forest!"

Nell watched Mark and Charlie select their climbing ropes and try on the harnesses for size. She shuddered. "Will we have to abseil again?" she asked Sensei Tanaka.

"Probably not, but you never know!" he said, "It is best to be prepared for all possibilities!"

Nell privately thought that this was a possibility she would rather not encounter again any time soon. She had been brave last time, but she wasn't keen to do it again. Nevertheless, she packed the equipment as the others had.

"How about food?" asked Mark. "What will we eat during the day?"

Sensei Tanaka laughed "A healthy boy has a healthy appetite! Fear not, young Mark. Food will be provided tomorrow morning and you can pack it in your food box - if you remember to pack it now!"

All the students scrambled to collect a food box to put in their rucksack. They didn't want to find themselves without anything to put food in to take with them tomorrow!

"And don't forget the water bottle!" called out Sensei Tanaka.

## Chapter 33

The students went off in their teams after collecting their equipment. Mark's team decided to go and lay their kit out as they had seen Sensei Tanaka do. They found a nice spot down by the river on the wide grassy expanse that lay in front of the main building. The four of them stretched out their groundsheets and unpacked their bags, laying out each item neatly in the same way that Sensei Tanaka had done.

James and Malcolm soon realised that they had neglected to collect climbing harnesses, although they had packed ropes.

"Do you think we really need a climbing harness?" asked James.

"Well, it would be bad luck if you didn't pack it and then we had to climb a tree or something. We don't know what we have to photograph yet!" said Mark.

"We had better go back and get the harnesses," said Malcolm.

James and Malcolm went off back to the stores to fetch harnesses for their packs. Mark and Charlie continued to check their kit.

"I think we have all we would need," said Mark "We will only be gone a couple of days and the camping equipment and most of the food will be provided. So we just need the basics really: map, compass, food box, water bottle, first aid, spare socks."

"What else could we possibly need?" asked Charlie

A voice appeared from behind them "I hope you packed the most important piece of equipment". It was Mr Liu. The boys jumped to their feet and said together "Hello Mr Liu!". They were very pleased to see him just before their big adventure.

"What's the most important piece of equipment Sir?" asked Mark

Mr Liu tapped the side of his head and winked. "Your brain!"

The boys laughed. "That lives in our head!" said Charlie.

"Well you had better not lose your head then!" said Mr Liu, chuckling "Or your heart! A warrior needs to have both and both must be strong."

"Mr Liu..." started Mark

"Yes, Mark?" Mr Liu encouraged

"What's the difference between a Ninja and a Warrior?" asked Mark "We are taught Ninja Skills, but it seems that the teachers here want us to be a Warrior rather than a Ninja. But no-one has really explained the difference."

"I am glad you asked that question. It is an important one." Mr Liu replied "It may take you a lifetime to entirely understand what it means to be a Warrior. We can teach you the skills of a Ninja, but becoming a Warrior is a journey for your own heart."

Mark and Charlie looked puzzled. They didn't really understand.

Mr Liu continued "Don't worry. It will take time for you to understand the difference. The Academy will teach you the difference. For now, you must just do your best and be your best."

"We have been doing our best," said Mark "I just hope our best is enough. I really want to be selected to be a student here."

"It all rides on the final assessment exercise tomorrow," said Charlie "We have to do well and get all those photographs!"

"I am sure you will," said Mr Liu "But remember! It isn't what you do that counts, it is how you do it."

"What do you mean Sir?" asked Mark, who was always pretty direct when he didn't understand something entirely. He found that asking questions was always the best way to end up understanding something.

"There are many ways to measure success. Different kinds of people measure success in different ways. How they measure success says a lot about the kind of person they are. I advise you young people to think very carefully about how you measure success. Ask yourself – what is important? What is good?" Mr Liu gave one of his mysterious smiles "If you do what you think is good and right, it will never matter how anyone else judges it. But make sure you know what is good and right."

Mr Liu chuckled "That can take a lifetime too! It would be so much easier if we were born knowing what is good and right!"

"My father said that the most important thing a police officer must do is care about people. Is that what you mean by what is good and right Mr Liu?" asked Mark.

Mr Liu gave Mark a slightly sad smile "Your father was a very great and wise man Mark. Caring about people is just about the most important thing there is. If you care about people, you will always do what is good and right."

"I wish you could come with us tomorrow Mr Liu!" piped up Charlie.

Mr Liu turned to Charlie "This is the first of many great adventures you must undertake on your own. But I know you will be most excellent!"

"Thank you, Mr Liu," replied both boys.

"Now I really must get on. I have an appointment with a rose bush," said Mr Liu.

"Do rose bushes make appointments?" asked Charlie in surprise.

"These ones do. They are tea roses!" Mr Liu wandered off laughing at his own joke.

**Chapter 34**

The following morning, the students were all up early. They ate a good breakfast and were assembled in front of the Summer Dojo at nine o'clock in the morning. Sensei Tanaka, Sensei Goodwin and Sensei Silver were all there waiting for them.

Sensei Silver walked amongst them, handing out a sheet of paper to each group. As he did so, Sensei Tanaka briefed them on the task ahead. "On the piece of paper that Sensei Silver is giving you is a list of things that you must take a photograph of. Each item may be found in the forest somewhere, if you know where to look and how to look!"

"The first item is a Spruce tree branch. Do not confuse this with a Pine tree or a Fir tree. It must be a Spruce tree. We will need to see a photo that shows the needles on the branch."

The students looked around at each other in alarm. The vast majority of them did not know the difference between a Spruce, a Pine and a Fir tree. Each of them hoped that someone on their team would.

"The second item is a white Deer. This will require great patience on your part. You must find a location where the Deer may like to wander and then you will have to wait with extreme Ninja quietness in order to get your photograph."

The students looked amazed at this. They had never heard of a Deer being white before. They thought it sounded very beautiful and magical.

"The third item is a river. We have been to the river together, so I hope you remember your Waymarks and Landmarks!"

"The fourth item is a Dragonfly. I will give you a little tip to help you find him. Ask yourself where Dragonflies like to go?"

"The fifth item on your list is a Calendula plant. Those of you who have made friends whilst you are here may find this easier to locate than others will."

"The sixth item on your list is photographs of the other teams. You have a choice here. You can either agree with the other teams to take photographs of each other. Or you can compete and try and take photographs of the others whilst avoiding being photographed yourselves. To make this fair, you cannot take photographs of the other teams until you have been in the forest for half an hour." he paused. "And we will know!"

The students smiled at each other. They had noticed that there wasn't much that happened in the forest that the instructors didn't know about. The forest had eyes everywhere!

"You will have two days to complete this exercise. You must make it to the old tower by six o'clock tonight. You will be met there with camping equipment and tonight's dinner. But you must carry your lunch with you. On the table over there..." he gestured to a long table that was laden with food "you may take whatever you like. Remember that you have to carry it though! So only take whatever food you think you will need to keep you going until dinner tonight. So go and choose your food now please."

171

Sensei Goodwin then went to each group and handed them a camera. "This camera is for the group to use. Be very careful not to lose or damage it. Obviously we want you to look after equipment belonging to the Academy, but also it will not be possible for us to extract and judge which photographs your group managed to take if you damage it. It is also important not to let the camera get wet. It will damage both the camera and the photographs if you do!"

Charlie nominated himself cameraman for the boys' group. He accepted the camera from Sensei Goodwin and put the strap around his neck. He felt very important with the camera hanging on his chest. He was really looking forward to taking these photographs. "Wouldn't it be amazing to take a photo of a white Deer?" he thought, hoping that he would be allowed to keep the photograph afterwards.

Xinia took the camera for the girls' group. She had a camera of her own at home and really liked taking photographs. What an opportunity to take some photos in this beautiful forest! She wondered whether it would be okay to take photographs of anything else whilst they were out there.

"Right then! Off you go! Remember – you can't photograph the other teams until you are half an hour into the forest. And if you don't want your team to be photographed, I suggest you go into stealth mode before that. We will meet you tonight at the Old Tower. Stay safe, look after your team and make us proud!" said Sensei Tanaka.

## Chapter 35

The students all marched off to the forest, grouped in their teams. The teams very quickly moved apart from each other. They had all decided that they were not going to co-operate with other teams to exchange photographs, so they were all very keen to get away from the other teams so that those other teams couldn't photograph them either.

Once they had put distance between themselves and the other teams, Mark's team came to a stop. They crouched down behind a giant fallen tree to make their plans.

Mark was always inclined to take control in most situations. This was his big opportunity to get selected for the Academy, which would take him along his path to becoming a police officer. He was taking no chances on this exercise! So he spoke first, determined to lead his team to success. "I think we should start with what is closest and what we know. Sensei Tanaka took us to the river. It isn't far away and we have Waymarks set up for it. So let's go and get that photograph first."

"And we can get the Dragonfly at the same time," said Malcolm, who was very interested in nature. Malcolm and James spent much of their spare time wandering in the Scottish Highlands so had grown up knowing the creatures of nature and their habitats. "Dragonflies are to be found by the river"

"Brilliant!" said Mark "That will be two from the list located very quickly. Then we just have to get the Spruce, the white

Deer, the Calendula and the other teams."

"We can identify the Spruce," said James "That won't be a problem."

"Oh good! That's a relief. I wouldn't know a Spruce if I ran into one" giggled Charlie "and I probably would run into one!" The boys laughed.

"Well make sure you don't run into any trees whilst wearing the camera!" warned Mark.

"Just a thought..." said Malcolm, who was quite a strategic thinker. "If we are thinking of going to the river first, the chances are that the other teams will too. So if we were to go into stealth mode, we could creep up behind the other teams and photograph them whilst they are photographing the river and maybe the Dragonflies. They wouldn't even know it!"

"And when they have all gone, we can get our photographs of the river and Dragonflies too!" finished Mark "Great plan!"

The boys all nodded eagerly with excitement.

"I remember Sun Tzu saying something about the importance of arriving on the battlefield ahead of your enemy," said Malcolm "We had better get to the river and hide so we are in place to spy on the other teams."

"The others aren't our enemies though," said Charlie "Some of them are our friends"

"Today they are the competition," said Mark with determination "Let's go!"

The boys streamed through the forest, moving as fast as they could but staying quiet and hidden amongst the trees and away from the main path as much as possible, whilst still checking for the Waymarks they had set on their previous journey this way.

When they got close to the river, they could see the girls' team had arrived there first. Mark signalled the team to drop to the ground and stay out of sight. All four boys lay down in the undergrowth, but Charlie crawled carefully forward and snapped a photograph of the girls' team as they peered into the river looking for Dragonflies. What none of them noticed was that Xinia was above them, perched in a tree, which gave her the perfect vantage point to take a photograph of the boys' team as they lay amongst the bracken. She giggled to herself as she snapped the photograph. She couldn't wait to tell them about it later. The boys would be mad!

Having successfully laid the trap for the boys, Lucy, Nell and Gina set off, leaving Xinia in the tree. As previously arranged, they laid a series of Waymarks for her to follow. Once they were about ten minutes down their path, they stopped and hid behind some fallen trees. They were keen to avoid letting the other teams photograph them whilst they waiting for Xinia to catch up.

The boys meanwhile continued to lay in wait for the other teams. After a while, they began to realise that the other teams had decided to take a different route and maybe were going to pursue the items on the list in a different order.

"Let's get our photographs here and move on," said Mark "I don't think the other teams are coming yet."

Charlie went to the river and took a photograph of the water running downstream. Then he and the others lay down by the river's edge, looking for Dragonflies. It wasn't long before their efforts were rewarded. Actually getting a photograph of the Dragonflies wasn't so easy because they were moving around quite quickly. But one landed on a leaf that was floating down the river and this gave Charlie an opportunity to get the photograph.

"Hurrah! All done!" said Charlie.

"Well done Charlie," said James "Now let's go and find some Spruce trees. I remember passing some near here."

James led the boys' team back down the track they had taken to the river and off towards the area where he remembered seeing the Spruce trees.

"Ah hah! I thought so. Here is one" said James. Malcolm agreed with him "Definitely. Get the photo, Charlie"

"How do you tell the difference between a Spruce, a Fir and a Pine tree?" asked Mark who had grown up in an area where none of these trees were very plentiful.

"Well the first thing to do is look at how the needles are attached to the branch," said Malcolm "If they are attached in clusters, it is a Pine tree. The Spruce and Fir tree have their needles attached individually."

"So how do you tell the difference between the Spruce and Fir? Are you sure this isn't a Fir? Sensei Goodwin said that it absolutely has to be a Spruce tree that we photograph." said Mark, who was determined that they wouldn't make any mistakes and not win the challenge.

"Ah, well then you have to look at the needles" replied James "Fir needles are flat but Spruce needles are round. Well actually they are more square-like, but you can roll them between your fingers easily".

The boys each plucked a needle off the tree and rolled it between their fingers. "Yes! This is definitely a Spruce tree then!" said Mark, pleased.

Charlie took a photograph, making sure the photograph showed the detail of the needles, their shape and how they were arranged on the branch. "That should do it!" he said.

"We have four of the six items already!" said James "That's good progress. We haven't even had lunch yet! We have another team, the river, the Dragonfly and the Spruce"

"We only have one of the three other teams," said Mark "And come to think of it, there were only three girls by the river. I didn't see Xinia there. Did any of you?". The boys shook their heads.

"I am not sure if the photo will count if we don't get Xinia. I think we should put the other teams back on our list of things to photograph. So that means we still have to get the other three teams, the Calendula and the white Deer." Mark counted off the items on his fingers.

"My father often talks about low hanging fruit," said James "It means that when you have a load of things to do, you can start by doing the easy things and things that you know how to do before tackling the harder things and things that you don't know how to do. Perhaps we should go for the low hanging fruit here?"

"Like apples?" said Charlie, who was not entirely grasping this concept.

"No," said James "I mean we should think about what remains on our list and decide if we know how to get any of these items."

"Teams, Calendula, white Deer" listed Mark thoughtfully "Where have I heard that name Calendula before?" He scratched his head, hoping that would help him remember.

"Ah hah! I remember!" he exclaimed, "Do you remember when we helped Mrs Green with her shopping and she gave us lemonade and biscuits?" The boys nodded.

"Well, Lucy pointed out a plant in her garden and said that her mother uses it for medicine. I am pretty sure she said it was Calendula!"

Malcolm nodded "I do remember Sensei Goodwin saying something about people who had made friends would find this easier to locate. That must have been what he meant!"

## Chapter 36

After the boys had left the river, Xinia had lowered herself from the tree using her rope and climbing harness, using the single rope method that allowed her to easily retrieve her rope. Then she packed it back in her rucksack and followed the path that her team had marked for her. It didn't take her long to reach a small cone of sticks, which was the Waymark they had agreed for a meeting point. She grinned as the other girls slipped out from behind the fallen trees nearby.

"Did you get it?" asked Lucy.

"Oh yes!" said Xinia with glee "The boys have no idea I photographed them!"

"We had better hurry," said Lucy, "I think I pointed out the Calendula at Mrs Green's house to Mark when we were there. He has an awfully good memory. I think he would remember it. So we had better try and get there first so they can't ambush us and get a photograph of our team when we approach Mrs Green's house."

The girls set off together at a good pace and made it to Mrs Green's house around lunchtime. They knocked on the door.

"Oh hello!" Mrs Green said when she answered, "How nice to see you again!"

"Hello Mrs Green," said Lucy "We are doing a treasure hunt for the Academy and we have to photograph a Calendula as one of the items on our treasure list. I remember you have some in your garden. Would you mind if we photograph them please?"

"I would be delighted," said Mrs Green "take your photograph by all means. But it is lunchtime now and you all must be starving. Would you like to come and have some biscuits and lemonade in the back garden? You are in luck – I baked biscuits again today. It's almost as if I knew you would be visiting". She chuckled. Lucy suspected that she had been expecting them in fact. She had lived at the Academy long enough to know how things worked.

"Yes please Mrs Green!" said the girls, who were all very hungry now after their long walk through the forest.

Mrs Green invited them to go round the side of the house to the back garden where she brought them out a tray of biscuits and lemonade. The girls fell on the biscuits and ate them ravenously. They were so delicious and they were all very hungry. They were sitting on the grass relaxing and resting when there was a knock at the front door of the cottage. Mrs Green excused herself to go and answer it.

At the front door were Mark, Charlie, James and Malcolm. "Hello Mrs Green!" said Mark "Would you mind if we photographed your Calendula plants for our treasure hunt at the Academy, please? I remember Lucy pointing them out in your garden. Were they those little orange flowers over there?"

Mrs Green laughed "Of course you may and yes, those are the Calendula. As it happens, you are not the only ones wanting their photograph today!"

"Really?" said Mark "Did the girls come here too?"

"Yes, they are in the back garden having biscuits and lemonade at the moment," said Mrs Green "Would you like to join them? You must be rather thirsty and hungry."

The boys were indeed hungry. But Mark spotted an opportunity here to both get the photographs they needed and get ahead of the girls. He also didn't want to give the girls the chance to photograph them or hang around in case any of the other teams remembered there were Calendula here.

"That's very kind Mrs Green," he said "But we are in rather a hurry. We will just take our photographs and get along if you don't mind?"

"Of course! Of course! I understand entirely. Come back another day for lemonade and we can have a nice chat when you have more time" she said with a warm smile and went back indoors.

Charlie went and photographed the Calendula, admiring the pretty orangey-yellow flowers as he did. Then he slipped stealthily around the side of the house and snapped a quick photograph of the girls drinking lemonade on the grass. They didn't notice him.

The boys slipped away quietly. When they got a distance away, they burst out laughing. "The girls have no idea that we got their photo!" said Charlie.

"Well done Charlie!" said Mark. They all laughed and slapped Charlie on the back.

Meanwhile, the girls were still enjoying their drinks and snacks and chatting with Mrs Green. It was another twenty minutes or so before Mrs Green happened to mention that the boys had been at the door wanting to photograph the same Calendula flowers that they had.

"Oh no!" said Xinia "They will be ahead of us now. We had better hurry and catch up!"

The girls all thanked Mrs Green very politely and sincerely for the lovely biscuits and lemonade.

"Do come again!" Mrs Green called after them as they set off again.

## Chapter 37

"When is lunchtime? I'm starving!" said Malcolm. "Me too!" said James and then Charlie.

"Let's try and get to the big heathland before we stop for lunch. That's where we will stand a good chance of spotting the white Deer and maybe the other two teams! It would be so good if we got all our photographs on the first day!" said Mark.

"Okay, but I hope it isn't too far from here" grumbled Charlie "I am going to pass out if I don't have lunch soon!"

"You'll be fine," said Mark "It's not a lot further and I think you can wait just a little bit longer for your sandwiches. If we can get there, we can sit and eat our sandwiches whilst waiting for the other teams and the white Deer."

The boys agreed this was a good idea although they were all very keen to have their lunch. So they kept on trudging up the forest path in the direction of the big heathland. After a while, the path led to a clearing in the woods and in the middle of that clearing was an old man with a shabby tent and a wooden cart. Clearly he was a tramp of some sort and that wooden cart carried his belongings. He was rifling through the cart, looking for something.

"Good afternoon Sir," said Mark "Are you okay? You look like you are searching for something."

"Oh hello there!" said the old man "I was just looking to see if I had any food left. I am sure I had a crust of bread in here from yesterday but I can't seem to find it."

He kept on looking. It was obvious that he was hungry. The boys all looked at each other.

"We were about to stop for lunch," said Mark "Perhaps you would like to share lunch with us?"

"Well I am not sure I can find anything to share," said the old man sadly.

"That's fine Sir," said Charlie "We have plenty to share!"

In fact, they didn't have a lot to share because they had done as Sensei Tanaka had advised and only brought as much food as they thought they would need. They hadn't planned for feeding a hungry old man as well! But they were all nice and kind boys who thought of others before themselves, so they didn't let on and instead pretended they had plenty to share.

"That's very kind young Sirs," said the old man "Then let's sit together and you can tell me all about your adventures today. I assume you are out on an adventure?"

"Oh yes!" said Mark "We are on a treasure hunt. We have to photograph all these things in the forest."

"What do you have left on your list?" asked the old man.

"We just have to photograph two of the other teams and a white Deer," said Charlie.

"Oh! The white Deer!" chuckled the old man "You will have a fine time looking for him. He doesn't appear to order and you won't find him where you think you might."

"We were going to try the big heathland just north of here," said James.

"If you were covered in bright white fur, would you graze in a big open heathland where you can be seen for miles around?" said the old man.

"I hadn't thought of that," said Mark "Where would we find him do you think?"

"If I were you, I would be looking in the thickest part of the forest. He can hide much better there" replied the old man.

"Thank you Sir!" said Mark "That will really help us. Please have a sandwich" he offered him sandwiches from his lunch box and the old man gratefully accepted one.

"Would you like one of mine?" asked Charlie, offering his box as well.

"Well now, I wouldn't want to over-eat would I?" said the old man with a smile "When you get as old as me, you don't want to eat so much. But this sandwich here is very nice, very nice indeed. Thank you!"

The boys stayed and chatted with the old man a little longer whilst they ate their lunch. Then they got up to leave.

"We really must be going now. It was nice to meet you Sir!" said Mark. They all smiled and waved and then took their leave of him, following Mark off along the path.

"So we aren't going to find the white Deer at the big heathland," said James.

"But the other teams don't know that," said Mark "So let's go hunt them first. If we can get them this afternoon, that will leave all of tomorrow to head into the deepest parts of the forest to photograph the white Deer."

"Good plan!" cried Charlie with enthusiasm. He was feeling much better now that he had had his lunch.

The boys made their way through the forest north to the big open heathland. As they approached it, they slowed down. They knew they could run into the other teams now and this was their objective. They wanted to get photographs of the other teams whilst they themselves were waiting for the white Deer. They spread out along the edge of the opening, each of them finding a spot to drop down and wait. This also had the advantage of making their own team harder to photograph, because they were not close together anymore.

They couldn't see any of the other teams in the heathland itself. Through a series of gestures that Sensei Tanaka had taught them during Ninja Skills training, they agreed to spread out around the edge of the heathland. If the other teams were here, the chances were that they too were in place around the edge. Mark and Charlie went one way around the heathland and James and

187

Malcolm went the other. A couple of hundred yards around, Mark and Charlie spotted an observation deck. It was a deck of wood raised up about twenty feet and accessed by a ladder. Mark and Charlie dropped down into the undergrowth to observe it more carefully. They could see there were people up there. Charlie adjusted the lens on his camera so he could look in close at what was up there.

"It's David's team!" whispered Charlie.

"Brilliant! Get the shot!" said Mark.

"Click!" went the camera. The boys giggled and withdrew, heading back to where they had left James and Malcolm. After a while, the other boys returned to them. "We got David's team!" said Charlie. "Excellent!" said James and Malcolm.

The boys agreed to spend a couple of hours waiting to get the last team here before heading off to the Old Tower for the six o'clock rendezvous with Sensei Tanaka. So they spread out and sat amongst the bracken and behind trees in hope of getting the last photograph that they needed of the teams.

When it was about five o'clock, Mark looked at his watch and shook his head. "I think we need to give up on this for now and make our way to the Old Tower."

"Oh yes!" said Charlie "We don't want to miss dinner!"

The boys all agreed that missing dinner would be a terrible thing indeed and set off in all haste to make sure they got to the Old

Tower in time.

"But be careful!" said Mark "The other teams will be looking out for us to get our photograph too!"

**Chapter 38**

The four teams arrived in good time at the Old Tower. Waiting for them was Sensei Tanaka, the senior students Bella and John and a cook from the Academy. The cook had a barbeque already set up and a trestle table laid out with salads and bread. Once the students arrived, he started cooking slices of zucchini, aubergine, peppers, slabs of marinated tofu and various other tasty things.

The students tucked into their dinner. Mark decided to try houmous, asparagus and grilled peppers, with lashings of salad in a big bread bun. It was delicious!

"You have got to try this!" said Mark to Charlie.

"No thanks, I am on falafel, tomato and houmous" replied Charlie "It's gorgeous!"

The girls' team came over and joined them. "Did you have a good day?" asked Lucy.

"Great thanks!" replied Mark "We got loads of the photographs we needed. We just have Alicia's team and the white Deer left to do."

"We just have one team and the white Deer left," said Lucy "But we have all tomorrow to do that and it will involve going to a different part of the forest, so it made sense to get all the other items on the list in this area today."

"We had lunch with an old man who told us that too," said Charlie "Where will you be going?"

Lucy thought a moment and considered not telling them. She had an advantage because she had grown up in this area and knew where many things were to be found. But she wanted the boys' team to pass the assessment exercise too because they were her friends.

"We will head to the south-west area of the forest. It's very dense there and I know the white Deer is more likely to be found in that area. We have to be careful though. It's quite a dark and secluded area. The ground is hard to navigate in places too. There are boggy areas and some steep banks, almost like cliffs in places. So we have to pick our route and location carefully."

The other teams were listening in whilst Lucy told the boys about the best place to find the Deer. They decided that they would follow Lucy's team tomorrow.

After dinner, Sensei Tanaka and the senior students helped them put their tents up. There were enough tents for them to share, two to a tent. They pitched them around in a circle and made them comfortable inside with bedding which they chose from the large van that Sensei Tanaka had arrived in.

"It's another big day tomorrow!" said Sensei Tanaka "So make sure you get to sleep early and have a good night's sleep. You have one day left tomorrow to do something that will determine the path of the rest of your lives. Do well! Make us proud!"

There was a lot of whispering and giggling as the students settled down. By nightfall, all was silent. Sensei Tanaka sat nearby, watching the stars. He saw a shadowy figure move away through the trees. He clearly knew who it was though because he smiled and nodded his head to him.

# Chapter 39

At Shadowlands, it was the night before a big training exercise. The students were all excited. They knew they would be doing something important tomorrow, but hadn't been told what it was yet. They were all assembled in one of the training huts. Instructor Adams stood with his arms folded, ready to address them.

"Tomorrow is a very important day!" he said "You will be doing a training exercise that will prepare you for an extremely important future operation. So this is a practise run, but it will be in real conditions and it is absolutely imperative that you make no mistakes and you achieve the objective."

The ninja students all looked at each other, wondering what that would be. He continued.

"Your objective will be the capture of certain targets. The targets are the students from the Academy. They will be out in the south-west of the forest tomorrow, quite close to here in fact. You must capture a bunch of them, bring them back here and hold them in this hut overnight."

He picked up a long ruler and gestured to a large map that was pinned to a board. "You will fan out around this area. You will locate your targets, capture them, tie them and bring them back here. Do you understand?"

"Yes Sir!" they all said

"Now remember what you have been taught here. Effectiveness is key. You will be effective. You will be efficient. You will get the job done and you will get back here with no mistakes. Understood?!"

"Yes Sir" they all replied sharply.

"Now get to bed and report back here to get kitted up in the morning at first light," he said.

The students did as they were told. They filed out and returned to their bunkhouses. Pandora was quite excited. She knew she was training to be a ninja, but she hadn't expected a real operation like this so soon in her training! She realised that her sister Xinia would very likely be part of the Academy team and may be one of those that they capture. She sniggered "That will show her!"

## Chapter 40

The next morning, the student rose soon after sunrise, awoken by the light. Sensei Tanaka and the cook were waiting for them and helped them to a good breakfast. Then it was time to strike the camp, taking down the tents and tidying everything away.

"What's the first rule of camping?" asked Sensei Tanaka

"Leave no trace!" they all chorused, laughing as they tidied everything away. Once Sensei Tanaka was satisfied that there was not the tiniest sign that they had ever been there, he sent them on their way.

"But before you go..." he said, "I want you all to put your climbing harness on."

The students thought this was a strange direction, but they did as they were told.

"I know where many of you will be heading today and I think you will be needing to use your ropes in places. I don't want any of you hurrying to go down steep slopes and not using your harnesses. So better to put them on now so you don't try and save time by going down without them" he explained.

Once they had all got their harnesses out of their bag and clipped them on, they waved goodbye to Sensei Tanaka and set off.

Lucy's team went ahead first. The other teams hung back so they could follow but avoid being photographed once they got half an hour away from the campsite.

It was a long trek. They had camped in the north of the forest and had to make their way round to the south-west. As Lucy had said and Sensei Tanaka had suggested, the ground did in fact become increasingly hard to traverse. They found themselves picking around patches of wet, boggy ground and scrambling up and down some steep slopes. One slope, in particular, was very difficult to get up. Gina was not only an excellent gymnast but also a talented climber.

"I tell you what," she said "I will climb up and tie a rope up there for you all to use to help yourself up. It will be much easier for you with a rope. It's easy for me though because I do a lot of climbing, so I don't really need it."

Gina climbed the slope. It wasn't very high, only about twenty feet or so, but it was too far to fall. She moved steadily but carefully. When she got to the top, she fastened a rope around a tree there and threw the end of the rope down to the rest of the team.

Lucy was the first to follow. Using the rope to help her, she climbed the slope to the top. Xinia knew that Nell would find this hard, so she sent her up next. But Nell did well. Somehow it was easier to go up the slope than it would be coming down it. Xinia followed up the slope next and very soon all four girls had made it to the top.

Gina was about to untie her rope from the tree when Lucy stopped her. "Perhaps we should leave that for the others? They are bound to follow us and they might not have any good climbers like you in their team, Gina. I would hate them to have an accident and know that we could have prevented it."

Gina agreed "Yes, it would be a risky climb without a rope for someone who isn't used to it. Let's leave it for them. I don't want any accidents on my conscience! I would feel terrible if someone got hurt."

So the girls left the rope in place and it was very gratefully used by the other teams when they followed behind.

"Isn't that decent of them?!" cried Charlie.

"I remember Mr Liu saying it wasn't what you do that matters, it's how you do it," said Mark, "I think they did this very well indeed."

The boys all agreed the girls were jolly good sports for leaving the rope for them. They clambered safely up the slope, grateful for the rope's support.

They continued on, taking the main track away from the steep slope. It was another half hour or so when suddenly they saw Xinia running down the track towards them. She was crying and calling out to them "Help! Help!"

"What's happened?" asked Mark "Where is the rest of your team?!"

"They've been kidnapped!" cried Xinia "There was a team of young ninjas, about our age, all dressed in black. They put sacks over Lucy, Nell and Gina, tied ropes around them and dragged them off. I only escaped because I was hanging back hoping to get a photograph of one of the other teams."

"Oh no!" said Charlie "Who were they? Where did they take the girls?"

Xinia stopped crying a moment and said very sadly "I recognised one of them. It was my sister Pandora."

"Are you sure?" said Mark.

"Yes, I recognised her eyes and a lock of her gold hair. It was definitely her" said Xinia "It must be that new ninja school she started at. They must have made her do it."

"There's another ninja school?" asked Mark. This was news to him. All the boys looked surprised by this too.

"Yes. When I called my parents a few days ago, they told me that Pandora had gone to a new school, a school of ninjas. I didn't think to mention it" she replied.

"Well then, that's must be where they have taken the girls. Is it near here?" asked Mark

"Yes, I think so. My mother did say it wasn't too far from the Academy" Xinia recalled.

By this time, the other two teams had caught up with them and had heard what had happened. They were also quite pleased to have been able to snap a photograph of the boy's team whilst they were distracted. But Charlie was too worried about Lucy, Nell and Gina to think about photographing any of the other teams.

"We need to get after them," said Mark "The girls must be terrified!"

"We can track them through the forest," said James and Malcolm "On our Father's estate back home in Scotland we learned to track at an early age. We were normally tracking animals, so tracking humans will be even easier. Let's get going!"

Alicia's team shook their heads. "We aren't coming," said one of them. "It's their own silly fault for getting captured," said another. "We have to finish the exercise and pass the selection course," said Alicia.

David's team was of a similar opinion. But David, a big Welsh lad with a shock of blonde hair and a powerful presence, stepped forward. "I am coming with you Mark," he said, "We have to rescue the girls."

"But you have to come with us or you won't pass the test," said one of his team.

"Look here," he said "I am going to be a policeman one day. I wouldn't make much of a policeman if I didn't help when people are in trouble, would I? You do as you like, I am going with the lads to rescue the girls. But if you are going to do something useful, you could go straight back to the Academy and let the Senseis know what has happened."

With that, he set off up the path with Xinia, Mark, Charlie,

James and Malcolm.

## Chapter 41

Lucy, Nell and Gina were all very scared. One minute they had been happily walking along in search of the white Deer and the next moment a swarm of black-clad ninjas had descended and surrounded them from the trees. They had thrown black fabric sacks over their heads, wrapped ropes around them and dragged them off through the forest. The girls had stumbled and tripped through the forest for miles, unable to see where they were placing their feet or what direction they were being taken in.

Eventually, they had arrived at the place they were being taken to. They couldn't see where that was until they were taken inside some sort of room, untied and the sacks were removed from their heads. They appeared to be in a rough concrete classroom of some sort. The walls were covered in old, peeling paint and the window panes were cracked and old. There were some old metal chairs and a mattress on the floor.

"Where are we? What are you doing with us?" asked Lucy when their capturers took the sack off her head.

"Never you mind" came the reply from the ninja who seemed to be leading the group. Lucy thought she recognised the voice, but she couldn't place it.

"We need to get back to the others," said Nell "They will be worrying about us!"

The ninja looked at her a moment. Nell thought she saw a spiteful smile behind that mask even though she could only see the eyes. The eyes were slightly familiar, but Nell was so upset by her situation, she barely noticed.

"You are going to be here a while. Sit if you wish, lay down if you wish. It doesn't matter to me. But you will be staying in this room" said the lead ninja.

Then they left. The ninjas all went out of the room leaving Lucy, Nell and Gina alone.

"What should we do?" asked Nell, who was the most nervous of the three of them.

Gina looked at the rickety old windows "I reckon I could kick those windows out and we could climb out through there."

Lucy looked out of the window. There were ninjas placed all around the building. "No use, they have guards everywhere. We wouldn't get far before they caught us again" she said.

"I think we had better stay put for a while," said Nell "We don't want to make them angry. They might hurt us."

"Well I doubt they will keep this level of guarding up all day," said Lucy "We could wait until they get bored or go to dinner or something and then try and escape."

The girls agreed this was a good idea. They settled down on the chairs and mattress and waited.

Meanwhile, Xinia and the boys were getting closer and closer to where they were being held. James and Malcolm had indeed turned out to be talented trackers. They had easily picked up the track made through the woodland by the troop of ninjas. Had they been more experienced and better-trained ninjas, this might have been impossible. But they were just students and had very little training, so they made quite a conspicuous track through the forest that was easy for James and Malcolm to follow.

Eventually, they came to the edge of the forest. Right ahead of them was a large military-looking training camp. It was the Shadowlands School of Ninjas, although it was not marked as such and the boys did not know it. But they could see the sort of place it was. Mark signalled to the team to fall back into the forest so they could make their plans.

"I reckon we should just march straight up to the front gate and tell the guard we are here for the girls. And if he doesn't play ball, we should just tackle him and force our way in" said David, who saw most things in terms of Rugby.

"I think that would give us away," said Mark. "I wonder if there is a way in through the fence?"

"If there isn't, we could cut our way in," said Malcolm "I brought wire cutters."

"Seriously? You brought wire cutters?" asked Charlie in amazement.

"Well, Sensei Tanaka said we could take whatever kit we wanted" explained Malcolm "and back home we always take wire cutters with us when we are out in the hills in case we have to cut an animal free of fencing or something."

"Well thank goodness for that!" said Mark "Yes, I think cutting our way in will be the best way. But first, we need to work out where to cut. So let's spread out and see if we can work out where the girls are being held."

They all spread out and took up positions along the forest edge at different places around the long fence that surrounded the training camp. After a while, Xinia spotted something very familiar. A ninja had walked out of a concrete building, taken off her ninja mask and shaken out her long wavy blonde hair. It was Pandora! Xinia gasped. She pretty much knew that it was Pandora she had seen earlier but it was still shocking to see it confirmed so clearly. She hurried back along the edge of the forest, gathering the others up as she went until they were all together again. She told them what she had seen.

"Then that's where we need to cut the fence and get in," said Mark.

"What will we do once we get in?" asked Charlie.

"There were a lot of ninjas on guard around that building," pointed out Xinia.

Mark looked at his watch "Well I make it just about lunchtime. I don't think they will all be out there much longer. So let's get in the place where we want to break in so we are ready when the time comes."

He was right. At half-past twelve, all except one of the ninjas drifted away to get their lunch, leaving just one on the door.

"Now!" said Mark. Malcolm crept out of the forest to the wire chain-link fence. He made short work of cutting an access hole in it. The other five of them were with him moments later. They all slid through the hole in the fence he had made. They had gone through the fence a little further on from the building that the girls were being held in so they could creep round past another building and not make a direct approach. They moved carefully with as much stealth as they could muster. At one point, they heard footsteps and voices nearby. They all rolled themselves up into silent, still, balls on the ground, remembering what Sensei Tanaka had taught them "Be a rock!" thought Charlie. He had never thought he would actually need to do that.

When the danger had passed, they moved on. James whispered to Mark "I think I see something – I have an idea. You lot go fetch the girls and Malc and I will check out that building over there. I think I can see motorbikes in it. They might come in handy if we have to leave in a hurry."

Mark, Charlie, David and Xinia carried on to the concrete building that the girls were being held in whilst James and Malcolm went to investigate the motorbikes. They managed to get to the window of the girls building without being seen by anyone. Fortunately, all the ninja students were at lunch. They looked in and were relieved to see Lucy, Nell and Gina sat there. Mark tapped very lightly on the window. The girls looked up and were delighted to see their friends there. Mark put his finger to his lips to warn them to be quiet. Then he pointed to first himself and then the door to let them know he would be coming to get them round there.

The next thing the girls knew, the door to their little prison was being opened and Xinia stood there. Mark and Charlie dragged the ninja guard in and tied him up and gagged him with the black silk scarves that they had been trained to always carry tucked into their belts. They were glad that they had heeded this training.

Having securely tied the guard to some pipework in the prison, they all crept out. At that moment, James and Malcolm appeared. "Guess what?" said James "Not only is that building full of motorbikes, they all have the keys in them."

"I am not sure we ought to take them. They don't belong to us" said Mark.

"The girls didn't belong to them either," said David "We need them to get away quickly and avoid all of us getting locked up here. It's self-defence!"

Mark looked doubtful but he had to agree it was the best way to get out of this place quickly and put a lot of ground between themselves and these bad ninjas.

So the students all crept over to the building with the motorbikes. Those that felt confident to ride one took one each and those who didn't climbed on the back of the bikes of those who were confident. Then they all fired up the engines and streamed out of the building they had found them in.

The noise of the bikes caught the attention of the ninjas and instructors in the dining hut. Instructor Adams looked out the window and immediately realised what was happening. He roared with anger.

"You useless lot! How could you let this happen?! Get after them!" he yelled.

The ninja students all scrambled to their feet and out of the door. Seeing the Academy students fleeing on their motorbikes, some tried to run after them and some ran to the bike building to claim the bikes that were left. They set off after them.

The Academy students were heading for the gate. A guard stood in his way, his arms wide to tell them to stop. They just streaked past him, riding either side of his outstretched arms.

Once free of the Shadowlands encampment, they headed into the forest. They knew they shouldn't take the bikes into the forest, but they had no choice. They didn't know if lives were at risk. They just knew that they had to get away from the ninjas who were now following them.

James and Malcolm led the way, each on a separate bike. They had led the way here and were best able to lead the way back. Mark and Charlie followed, sharing a bike. Then came Xinia, with Lucy riding behind her and Gina with Nell riding being her. David brought up the rear.

They made it as far as the steep slope that they had climbed up earlier. They skidded their bikes to a stop here. There was no way the bikes could go any further. They could hear their pursuers bikes heading towards them. There wasn't a lot of time. Gina's rope was still in place. They all were grateful at that moment that Sensei Tanaka had made them wear their harnesses for this exercise. So it was a moment's work to attach the harness and make their way down the rope.

Mark went down first. Meanwhile, Lucy pulled her climbing rope out of her backpack and Gina affixed it to another tree so that they had two ropes to go down and could all get down twice as fast.

James and Malcolm went down on the two lines together, moving quickly. Then David and Nell went. Nell hesitated a moment. She had been so frightened the last time she had done this. But this time the most dangerous thing was the possibility of getting captured again by the bad ninjas. She remembered what Sensei Tanaka had said and just took it a step at a time until she reached the bottom.

Last to descend were Charlie and Xinia. But the Shadowlands ninjas had caught up with them by now. Charlie and Xinia were halfway down their ropes when they looked up and saw the masked faces above them. Xinia looked up into the eyes of her sister, Pandora, burning with rage through the slit in her mask. The last thing she remembered was seeing a flash of metal as Pandora sliced a knife through the rope Xinia was climbing down.

Charlie stretched out to try and reach Xinia to stop her falling. But he couldn't. Moments later, he joined her abruptly at the bottom of the slope as his own rope got cut by a sadistically smiling Melissa. Melissa and Pandora looked at each other and laughed, very pleased with themselves.

Pandora had not thought through her decision to cut the rope. She may have been successful in hurting the Academy students, but she had also cut the rope and prevented her own teammates from following them any further. Once she realised her mistake she howled with anger and frustration.

At the bottom of the slope, Xinia lay unconscious and Charlie was chalky white. He had damaged his ankle and was in a lot of pain.

Lucy sprang into First Aider mode. She could see Charlie was hurt but conscious. Xinia was more of a worry. She lay there motionless. Lucy checked her breathing and pulse. They seemed fine. But she could see that Xinia had banged her head. "She must have hit her head and been knocked out," said Lucy "That's really dangerous. We need to get her back to the Academy as soon as possible."

Lucy checked Charlie. He had some minor cuts and scratches. She delved into her rucksack and produced some medicinal powders and a cloth. She dampened the cloth with water from her drinking bottle, then sprinkled the powders onto it and dabbed them onto Charlie's wounds to stop the bleeding. Then she collected ninja scarves from several of the team and used them to bind up Charlie's ankle. "There, that should give you a bit of support to help you get home," she said.

"Right," said Mark "I will carry Xinia. Can two of you support Charlie, please? We need to get them back to the Academy as quickly as possible. Are we ready to travel Lucy?"

Lucy nodded "We are as ready as we can be right now. But please hurry, I am so worried about Xinia."

Mark picked Xinia up, using the fireman's carry that Sergeant Yeald had taught him years ago. Normally he just practised it on his friend Geoff, but now he needed to use it for real. It wasn't very dignified for poor Xinia who was now slung around his shoulders, but it was the best way to get her back to the Academy as fast as possible.

So they limped along, Charlie strung up between David and Malcolm and Mark carrying Xinia, with James leading the way and Lucy constantly checking on the invalids. It felt like an even longer walk on the way back than it had on the way out. Mark found himself getting very tired and Charlie was wincing in pain.

But they kept going. Xinia's life might depend on it. They all realised that. Every time Mark felt ready to drop with exhaustion and aching legs and shoulders, he kept on going. Once or twice he thought he saw the dark shadow of an adult ninja through the trees, but he told himself he must be hallucinating because he was so tired and struggling to keep going.

Eventually, the Academy was in sight. Waiting for them were all the Senseis and Mr Liu, who was looking very concerned. Sensei

Silver took Xinia from Mark, who was very relieved to have the weight off his shoulders.

"Let's get them both to the doctor," said Sensei Goodwin.

Sensei Silver carried Xinia round to the back of the main building where the doctor had her office. James and Malcolm helped Charlie along behind. Lucy went too, to help her mother.

## Chapter 42

Mark and the others sat in the dining hall. The cook fussed around them, encouraging them to drink herbal tea and take some food. But they were all too worried about Xinia and Charlie to eat. Instead, they sipped at their tea and watched the door, waiting for news.

Eventually, the door opened and Charlie limped in. "I'm okay," said Charlie "My ankle isn't broken, it is just sprained."

"What about Xinia?" asked Mark anxiously.

"She is okay too. She has woken up. She has a bad headache of course and the doctor is keeping her in sickbay to keep an eye on her. But she should be fine by the morning."

"Oh thank goodness!" said Mark "I was really worried."

"Thank you for looking after me," said Charlie to them all. "I am just sorry we didn't manage to complete the treasure hunt."

"It wasn't your fault Charlie," said Mark, "It wasn't anyone's fault except the ninjas that captured the girls."

"If we hadn't let ourselves get captured, you wouldn't have had to rescue us and you might have finished the treasure hunt," said Nell guiltily.

"I am so sorry," said Gina "I know how important this was to you, to all of us in fact"

"I don't regret a thing," said Mark "My Father always said that the first priority of a Police Officer is preservation of life and it was a fabulous adventure too! Who knows if we would have passed this selection course anyway? And who knows what would have happened to the girls if we hadn't rescued them? At least we got to do something important. I am just glad it all worked out in the end. We got the girls back and Charlie and Xinia are going to be okay."

After having tea and something to eat, Mark and Charlie went outside to see Mr Liu. They knew they would be going home tomorrow so wanted to see him once more and say goodbye. They found him down by the river, wandering along with TigerLily.

"Hello, Mr Liu! We have come to say goodbye. We are going home tomorrow" said Mark.

"Oh that's nice!" said Mr Liu "But I am sure it won't be for long. You will be coming back for the start of the new school year and that's only a few weeks away."

Mark looked sad "We didn't finish the treasure hunt. It all went terribly wrong. The girls got captured by wicked ninjas and we had to go and rescue them. Then Charlie and Xinia got hurt when we were escaping and making our way back home. It was terrible! There is no way we will get selected now. Alicia's team and the rest of David's team finished the treasure hunt. They will be the ones that get picked."

Charlie looked miserable too. Now that it was all over and he was back safely, all he could feel was a sense of failure and a very sore ankle. He hung his head.

Mr Liu smiled at them kindly "Sometimes the things we think are important really are not. You can fail at one thing whilst succeeding at another."

"But we needed to succeed at the treasure hunt!" said Charlie

"I think you succeeded at what was important. You rescued your friends and you got everyone back home safely" replied Mr Liu. "Have faith! Don't you think your instructors here know what matters?!"

Mark and Charlie thought Mr Liu was being very kind to them, as he always had been/

"Thank you, Mr Liu," said Mark and Charlie together "Thank you for everything. Goodbye – and goodbye TigerLily!"

They turned and sadly made their way back to the house, Charlie leaning on Mark for support for his injured ankle. The Academy had never looked more beautiful now that they were about to leave it, for probably the last time. Mark desperately hoped that somehow the instructors would overlook their failure to get the last photographs. But he knew they couldn't.

Mark looked up at the magnificent old building wistfully, wishing it could become his home for the next five years or more. He had come so close to it. But he knew he had done the right thing. His Father would have valued what he had done much more highly than completing the treasure hunt. He wished he could tell his Father about it. He wished he could tell him everything. But he had grown up knowing that such wishes are fruitless and only lead to sadness. He also knew that the goodness of a person was measured by what they do when no-one is watching. His father had always said that becoming a good Police Officer begins with becoming a good person. Today he had done what he thought was the good and right thing to do. If that didn't lead to training to be a Police Officer here at the Academy, it was at least a good step towards becoming a Police Officer in a different way.

## Chapter 43

The Shadowlands students lined up on the training ground. Instructor Adams had been yelling at them for some time. His face red with anger, he continued to pace up and down the line of students, finding fault in each and pointing out what they had done wrong that day.

"Who here thought that guarding your prisoner involved wandering off for lunch?" he asked, daring each of them to admit to this.

"No one? No one at all? So no one here thought that when lunchtime came around, the best thing for them to do would be to go and get a meal?"

He stared into one face and then another. The students all stayed extremely quiet and just stared ahead, avoiding meeting his eyes.

"I have to wonder then, why our prisoners were suddenly left unguarded at lunchtime. I wonder about that a lot. In fact, I will be wondering about that all today, all of tomorrow and for quite some time to come. I will just be *wondering*!" He spat the last word out for emphasis.

"The next time you are asked to guard a prisoner, you will do just that. You will not wander off for lunch, breakfast or even High Tea. There will be no wandering at all. You will stand at your post and you will prevent your prisoner from escaping. That's rather the point of prisoners" he added sarcastically.

Eventually, he had walked off the worst of his anger. He stopped his pacing and stood in front of them. "Nevertheless, it was not an entirely incompetent performance. You at least managed to make the capture in the first place and were successful in bringing your prisoners here. I will give you a tiny bit of credit for being effective in this at least." He eyed Pandora and Melissa as he added "As you know, effectiveness is a core quality here. We don't expect much of you, but we do expect effectiveness. On this occasion, you showed enough to at least make your kidnap and extraction. We just need to work on your guarding skills."

A wicked smile came across his face "We can work on that for the rest of the day in fact."

"But before we get to that, I will also give you credit for giving chase to the escaping prisoners. Pandora in particular demonstrated admirable ruthlessness by cutting a climbing rope and sending her own sister falling. And Melissa cut another student's rope. That's the kind of teamwork and single-minded effectiveness we expect from Shadowlands students. No matter who it is and no matter how cruel the job you are sent to do, you must execute it with ruthless efficiency and without question. You don't have to like each other to operate well together. Well done Pandora and Melissa, I want to see more of that!"

Pandora smiled smugly. At last, she felt she was in a place where her talents were recognised and appreciated. She was beginning to enjoy her time at Shadowlands.

"Now," said Instructor Adams "It is time to work on your

217

guarding skills." He pointed to two of the students "You two! Go to the kitchen and ask the cook for a sack of potatoes. Then you are to take it to the training hut and tie it up. Then you can all spend the rest of the day guarding it. If you can successfully guard a sack of potatoes, we might try something more demanding tomorrow!"

## Chapter 44

The Senseis met that evening, clad in their long robes. As they sat around the luminous white table, they considered the array of student photos. They had divided them into two groups.

"I think we are agreed," said Professor Ballard.

"They made it very clear for us this year," said Sensei Tanaka.

"It's the easiest selection I can remember," said Sensei Goodwin.

The White Ninja said nothing but nodded. All the other Senseis nodded too and made noises of agreement.

"So that's that," said Professor Ballard, "I think the more concerning issue is that of Shadowlands. They have sabotaged our exercises before. It's almost a tradition. We expected it and prepared for it. But this is the first time they have gone as far as kidnapping our students and we haven't had students injured by them before."

"We had it all under observation of course," said Sensei Tanaka "The students had no idea they were being watched, but we monitored everything, saw the kidnapping, saw where and how the girls were being held. And we saw the boys and Xinia go to rescue them."

"We didn't expect what Pandora did though," said Sensei Silver.

"Unfortunately that wasn't completely surprising," said Sensei Goodwin "she has a vicious streak in her. That's why she couldn't stay here after all."

"Quite," said Professor Ballard "And she clearly has no love for her sister. What sort of girl would cut the rope her own sister was on, causing her to fall and get knocked unconscious. She might have killed her!"

"I think we know what sort of girl does that. That's why she was snapped up by Shadowlands" interjected one of the other Senseis.

Professor Ballard looked thoughtful "Pandora aside, we have to ask ourselves why Shadowlands is sending junior students out to practise capturing. That's an escalation, even by their standards."

"There is always a reason for the things they do. They are up to something" said Sensei Goodwin.

"I think it would be a good idea to keep a closer eye on the Shadowlands encampment," said Sensei Silver "I will attend to it".

"We all will," said Sensei Tanaka.

## Chapter 45

The following morning, all the students were asked to assemble in the dining hall. Xinia had recovered well from her accident and the Doctor was pleased with her. She was allowed to leave the sickbay and join the other students for this final stage of the selection.

Professor Ballard stood before them with a clipboard in his hands. Every student stared at the clipboard, knowing their fate was written there.

Professor Ballard cleared his throat and then spoke. "Well done for making it through this Selection Course. Not every student made it this far, so you are to be congratulated for that. No matter what the outcome is for you personally, I hope you have enjoyed your time here and learned some useful things.

He looked at his list "Now I am going to read out some names. If I call your name, I would like you to go through that door to the great hall where I will join you shortly. I should warn you all that you will not all be called."

Tense looks were passed between the assembled students. Each one listened anxiously to hear their name called. The Professor started calling names. First, he called Alicia and then each of her teammates. Mark's heart sunk. Alicia's team had completed the Treasure Hunt and returned first. Clearly that was what the Academy was looking for.

Then the Professor called each of David's team, but not David himself. This wasn't surprising as David had come on the mission to rescue the girls. David looked down at the floor miserably. He knew he had done the right thing, but it was still hard to be left behind when all the rest of his team were called.

Once David's team were called, the Professor walked out behind them, his clipboard still in his hands. He didn't even look back at Mark and the students who remained uncalled.

"Well that's that," said Mark and sat down heavily.

"Oh well, we did have a brilliant time here and an excellent adventure," said Charlie.

"Well it's back to Wales for me," said David "But at least I got to ride a motorbike through a forest!"

"And back to Scotland for us," said James and Malcolm.

Lucy looked the most distraught of all of them. "They will send me away now. I can't live here anymore now I didn't pass the Selection. I will have to go away to another boarding school." She looked close to tears but was bravely fighting them off. Xinia patted her shoulder reassuringly.

Gina and Nell looked resigned. They knew they had blown their chances when they allowed themselves to get captured. But it was still very sad now that it was happening. They were sorry too that they wouldn't see the new friends they had made anymore.

"We won't see each other anymore," said Gina sadly.

"We must keep in contact," said Nell.

The door opened and Professor Ballard reappeared. The students all stood up respectfully.

"I won't keep you in misery any longer," he said. "I would like to congratulate you all. You have all been selected to join the Academy."

The students looked at each other in amazement. They had heard his words but it took several seconds for them to sink in and be understood.

"We passed?" asked Charlie weakly. He didn't understand what was going on.

"Yes, you passed." said Professor Ballard "We called out the other students names so they could save face and walk out with their heads held high. But they were not selected."

He continued "You have been selected for various reasons. We have seen great bravery from many of you. We have seen leadership, tenacity, endurance and good judgement. Nell, we have seen how you are willing to conquer your fears and we have seen that you are a gentle and decent girl who will make a fine officer one day. Gina, you are a natural gymnast and athlete. You will make an excellent martial artist and a good team player, which is essential for the work we prepare you for."

"Lucy – dear Lucy, it can never have been in any doubt that you would become a student here. You share your Mother's gifts for healing and medicine and we are aware of your more unusual gifts of perception too. You will learn to refine and harness these here. Xinia, you are everything that your sister is not. You have impressed us from the moment you arrived. You are a gifted horsewoman like your Mother. I hope you will bring your own horse back with you when you return so you can continue your journey with him here."

Xinia's face lit up. Nothing could please her more than coming back here with her horse. She had been worrying about being apart from him if she was lucky enough to get a place at the Academy. But now she would be able to both study here and have her beautiful Rainbow with her! She couldn't be happier!

Professor Ballard smiled, pleased to see how happy Xinia was. He continued "And now for the boys!"

"David, you walked away from your team and joined the mission to rescue the girls. It takes great integrity and strength of character to do the right thing when those around you are not. You are also a bold and brave lad."

"James and Malcolm, your knowledge of nature has been of great use in this last exercise. You have also been excellent team members and are brave and strong too. You have made good choices on all of your assessment exercises – both the ones you knew about and the ones you didn't!"

"Charlie, you showed great skill at stealth and did well in your martial arts lessons. But most importantly, you never even questioned whether you should go and rescue the girls. You are brave and loyal and people will always want to know you and work with you."

"Mark, from the very first and every day since you have shown yourselves to be a natural leader and an even more natural Police Officer. Your father would be very proud of all you have done here and the outstanding way in which you led your team. You are brave and bold too, but your integrity shines out even more. You have done everything we could have wanted and much more."

Mark blushed scarlet, pleased and proud of the things that Professor Ballard had said about him.

"Now that you have all been selected, I must tell you a little more about what you have been selected for," said Professor Ballard.

"You probably think that this is just a training school for martial artists and prospective Police Officers. You will have worked out by now that it is more than a school for ninjas though. In fact, your recent brush with the students of Shadowlands School for Ninjas will have shown you some of the difference at least."

The students listened in carefully. "What was he saying?" they wondered.

"If you decide to take up the place that is being offered to you here, we will train you to become a Warrior of Light," he said. The students looked puzzled. They had no idea what he was talking about.

225

Professor Ballard smiled "I know, you don't know what that is yet, or what it involves. A warrior is so much more than a ninja. You will learn all the physical skills of a ninja of course, but a warrior is one with a code of ethics, a certain philosophy and way of living."

"We will only teach you what we believe to be good. We want you to become part of the forces of light and for your influence when you go out into the world to be one of goodness."

"You have all been chosen because you are fundamentally good and because you have certain talents and aptitudes. We think you can become great Warriors of Light if you undertake to train with a committed heart for the years ahead of you. The question is – do you accept that invitation?"

Nine eager faces looked up at him "Yes Sir!" they all cried in unison.

## Chapter 46

It was hard saying goodbye to all his new friends, but Mark knew it was only for a few weeks.

"Write to me every week!" said Charlie to him.

"Of course! And you write to me too!" replied Mark.

Mark was just about to get into the minibus to go to the railway station when he spied Mr Liu and TigerLily nearby. "Mr Liu!" he cried "We made it! We will be back in a few weeks!"

Mr Liu gave Mark and Charlie a big grin. He had known of course, but he was delighted to see how happy the boys were. TigerLily gave them a loud whickering sound.

"Bye TigerLily!" called Mark "See you at the beginning of term!"

The boys clambered into the minibus and took seats in the back row. As it drove off down the driveway, they looked back at the magnificent building that would be their home for the next five years. Lucy was standing at the top of the drive waving them off. They waved back and called "Bye Lucy!" even though she couldn't hear them in the minibus.

The journey home went by in a blur. Mark's mother was waiting for him in London.

"I made it Mum! They selected me! Gosh, I have missed you so much!" he said to her and gave her a big hug.

She hugged him tightly. "I've missed you!" she said "And of course they selected you. You are my son and your Father's son. There was no question about it" she said proudly.

In the days that followed, Mark told his Mother about everything that had happened whilst he was at the Academy. She was amazed to hear about his daring rescue mission.

"Goodness! You have had some big adventures! You must tell Sergeant Yeald about them. He will love to hear about it all. I tell you what, I will invite him over for tea."

She was as good as her word. The very next day Sergeant Yeald came to tea when he finished his shift. He listened with a broad smile as Mark told him about everything he had learned, about Mr Liu and TigerLily, about returning the lost dog to her owners and about the dramatic incident during the final assessment exercise, rescuing the girls, riding a motorbike through the forest and then carrying Xinia back to the Academy.

When Mark told him about how Professor Ballard had called the names of the students who didn't make it first, Sergeant Yeald chuckled "They are still doing that old trick are they?!"

"Did they do it to you too?" asked Mark

"Oh yes! It's a tradition" said Sergeant Yeald "It lets the ones who don't make it down gently and gives you a few minutes to consider the line between failure and success. That's an important lesson, that line is like the line between life and death. It's very fine and far too easy to fall the wrong side of it."

228

At that moment, the phone rang. "Excuse me," said Mark's mother and went to answer it. She returned a moment later. "Mark, it's for you. It's the Academy."

Mark went to the phone. When he returned he looked surprised and excited. "That was the Academy. Something important has come up and they need all the students to return as soon as possible."

Sergeant Yeald smiled "And so your adventures continue young Mark!"

THE END

# COMING SOON!

## *MARK VARDY*
### *AND THE*
### *POLITICIAN'S DAUGHTER*

Mark Vardy and friends return for a new adventure at The Academy!

## ABOUT THE AUTHOR

C.J.T. Wilkins is a Martial Artist and instructor, living in the New Forest, Hampshire, England.

A wearer of many hats.

Printed in Great Britain
by Amazon

58134228R00137